THEY ARE CURSED LIKE YOU

TRAILER PARK WITCHES BOOK I

BY HOLLEY CORNETTO & S.O. GREEN

Eerie River Publishing

Box 99900 HP 157 673

RPO Stanley Park

Kitchener, Ontario, N2A 0H1

Canada

Eerieriverpublishing.com

ISBN 978-1-998112-02-9

This manuscript is a work of fiction. In the novel, alongside characters who are pure fantasy and are products of the imagination and do not constitute a reconstruction of actual events.70

Edited by David-Jack Fletcher
Jr. Editor S.O. Green
Cover Design Luke Spooner

https://carrionhouse.com/

THEY ARE CURSED LIKE YOU

TRAILER PARK WITCHES BOOK 1
BY HOLLEY CORNETTO & S.O. GREEN

EERIE RIVER PUBLISHING
KITCHENER ONTARIO

Dedications

To Chris, for helping me figure out who I wanted to be.
- Holley

For John, who only cares about the important stuff.
- Simone

PROLOGUE

Four Rabbits

When they ran Belladonna Mason out, it was literal. They chased her into the woods wearing nothing but the shift her lover had bought her, so she could better play the part of the adulteress. And when his cuckolded wife caught them in the act—sinning against her and God in equal measure—he shed his loyalty to her just as easily.

Because "bewitched" sounded so much finer to his ears than "weak".

Though they'd cast her out and her home was gone and her name was ruined, she pushed on. Living was an awful difficult habit to break.

The woods had no love for her either. Stones cut her feet and every tree limb whipped her arms and back and thighs bloody and raw, like the preacher had when he found out. She was angry before, but the cold of the night and the lengthening shadows stole the heat from her. Even rage couldn't warm her.

And, when she fell in the mud, the last drop of strength trickled from her. They had bled her dry—this world and all the

people in it. She had no more tears to cry.

In the depths of the forest, beyond the limits of hope, was a fire crackling and the smell of meat cooking to put the edge on her hunger until it sliced across her belly. Slowly, she stood and walked and *wanted*. The human died there in the mud. The animal took over.

Funny how things worked out. She'd fled the fire, and fire was all that awaited her. She'd fled a man and there, upon a fallen tree, a man sat.

"Take a seat," he said. Not a request.

Belladonna's eyes didn't leave the meat—looked like rabbit—spitted over the flames. Not until she was sat, and the pain of her wounds and the warmth brought her back alive, did she finally see the man.

Handsome? Enough, though she'd tired of handsome men somewhere in the woods back there. Lean and muscled, furred with coarse, black hair. Eyes in shadow, reflecting the flickering firelight, or maybe just matching it. Stripped to the waist, dressed only in sack cloth. Staring.

Now, the cold had already made Belladonna quite aware of how thin her shift was, and this man was taking pains to remind her that the dangers of the woods weren't limited to things that howled and hissed.

"Hungry?" he asked.

She nodded. Words had betrayed her already, so many times. He didn't ask her to speak, just lifted a spit from the fire and pressed it into her hands. She tore flesh from bone and sobbed around every mouthful.

Still staring.

"You're not going to eat?" she asked, because betrayal hadn't ever taught her a lesson before.

He smiled. "Not yet."

Belladonna had never been under the presumption that

living in the woods was easy, but that smile had an ease to it that it shouldn't. And it was sharp, not just around the eye-teeth.

"You're awful far from home."

"I don't have a home."

She thought she heard a growl from the tree line. Something hungering for what she held in her hands. God told them not to covet but his creatures coveted plenty.

Then she realized it was him. Chuckling.

"You knew he was married," he said. "You knew she was spiteful. No one to blame but yourself."

Her turn to stare. He welcomed her gaze like a valley in spring. Oh, she could look around all full of wonder if she liked. When winter came, she'd never be able to leave.

"H-how do you know that?"

"I know a lot of things."

"Why are you talking in riddles?"

"Because you're not paying attention." He leaned across the fire and pulled the spit from her unresisting hands. The rabbit was bones now. He replaced it with another. Her hunger demanded another sacrifice.

"Who are you?"

"Not who."

"What are you?"

"A better question."

Of course. Because a man would need furs in this cold wilderness. A man would need a sword or a dagger. A gun. He would need a bedroll, a shelter. All this creature had was fire and meat.

Belladonna tossed aside the second stick, heard the bones rattle among the leaves like dice, and took a third. "Are you... human?"

"Not as such."

"Then why take a man's shape?"

She was of the opinion that there were more flattering shapes

to take, but the recently burned were most afraid of flames. Frankly, she'd rather have been anything else in that moment. A bird could fly away. A wolf could run without fear of cutting its pads to bloody shreds. A fish could swim wherever the river carried it.

Maybe not a rabbit though.

"There were no shapes for me to take in nature. I'm not the grass, trampled beneath your feet. I'm not the trees that shelter you. I watch all that passes, but I'm no raven. I hunger, but I'm no wolf. But a man? A man has needs he can't explain. A man needs to be worshipped. A man needs to stretch himself to fill all that surrounds him. A man needs to be a master. So, when your people breathed my air and stirred my soil and slaked their thirst from my rivers, I sat in their lungs and their hearts and their bellies and realized...I am a man also."

She had started and finished her fourth rabbit when he rose from his log and walked to her. His feet trampled embers. His eyes still glowed. The spit fell between her feet. Bones in the soil.

"And a man needs a woman." He reached for her cheek.

She shirked back, covering herself with her arms. "Not me."

Hadn't she suffered enough at the hands of men? Didn't her arms and legs and back bear their brutality? She had bled for their sins.

She didn't want to bleed for his too.

"If not you, then who? Don't you believe in fate? Don't you have quaint little notions of destiny and predetermination? And here you are, walking through my woods, sitting by my fire, eating up my rabbits. You're content to take but you won't give. That's not right, is it? Not right at all."

"M-maybe I'm here for a different reason."

The greatest portion of Belladonna's hate had always been reserved for Belladonna. The woman with no prospects who would go to the New World. The woman without a husband, even

where the men were plentiful and the women already betrothed. The woman who'd allowed herself to believe it meant something, even when he'd looked away in church.

The woman who couldn't look the Devil in the eye without cowering.

He tilted his head, curious. Like another man, she had a hook in him. She could only hope it was deeper this time around. "Maybe I can give you something else. Something more valuable."

"Like what?"

"What if I... What if I bring them to you? Others?"

He didn't answer. His attention was the held breath before a snare tightened. The moment a neck could break. The heartbeat as a flame caught or guttered out.

Life. Or death.

Her words spilled into the empty space and sloshed and gurgled until it overflowed. "You said you needed to be worshipped. You said you needed to fill this space. You said you needed to be a master. Let me help. I can help."

"How?"

"I know what to do. I've *always* known what to do, I was just..."

Weak. Always weak.

"I just never had the power. I could borrow some of yours and I could..."

Words dried up before they could nourish the unnamable sin. Her lips trembled and her eyes fell away, but he caught her chin, because she needed to see, and she needed to understand *exactly* what she was agreeing to.

"You owe me four rabbits," he told her.

And, because words had betrayed her, she nodded and said nothing.

CHAPTER 1

WHEN THE LUCK RUNS OUT

I don't know how old Belladonna Mason really is. Only that my grandparents knew a raven-haired beauty who lived in that venerable old house, with heels for walking on folks and a smirk on her ruby lips, and if that don't sound just like her.

And they used to warn me. *You stay away from that house, Loretta Dandridge, and don't you take nothing from the women who live there. They ain't no good.*

Well, as it turns out, there's only one woman who lives there. Belladonna. Our coven mama.

They built the Mason House out of the mountain, some good centuries ago. Was she around back then too?

They ground the earth's bones to lay the foundation, carved its forests to stumps and stains for timber, pressed its slippery flesh into molds and scorched it to erect walls. The ivy and the willows cling to it like children to their mother's tomb.

Or like parasites. One or the other.

Kind of the same way we cling to Belladonna, I guess. She's so much older and wiser than us.

Oh, she doesn't look it—the windows are clear and the veranda's swept clean and there's a fresh coat of whitewash on the walls—but it's there in that old country accent she can't quite shake. Like when she calls it "the wireless", or in the way she styles her hair, like Marilyn don't care no more if gentlemen prefer blonds.

They *let* Belladonna walk on them. The alternative doesn't bear thinking about. Any girl who saw the shit she got away with would want to know how she did it. That was how she got the hook in us to begin with, back in the 90s, when she'd invited us up to the old place for "Bible study". I drank my first glass of wine in Belladonna Mason's kitchen. I kissed my first girl—not Belladonna—in Belladonna Mason's parlor.

We killed a rabbit in the parlor too, crying and shaking from it, and touched each other's foreheads with bloody fingers. The wine didn't help. Belladonna had smiled at us, gathered us in her arms, told us to wash up while she finished.

I still wear my rabbit foot. We all do when we're at the House. I don't like to when I'm home though. It sends a shiver of agony through my soul whenever the fur touches my skin.

I think maybe Belladonna likes the agony.

"And how are my favorite students this afternoon?" she asks, stepping out onto the veranda—we'd become increasingly brazen since the millennium—with a bottle and a glass for each of us.

Wine, women, and witchcraft. One of her favorite recipes. There were others, of course. Potions to arouse, to repulse, to turn cancer into nothing and nothing into cancer. I'd tried to make them myself—pretty sure we all had—but it didn't work the same alone. Only the coven had the power.

It kept us coming back. Kept us clutching our feet.

"Anais has a love rival," I grin.

Belladonna arches an eyebrow, always enthralled by the sordid. "Oh? Don't keep me in suspense, Loretta."

"Super Bowl season," Anais grumbles. "I think I'd prefer if Marty had an affair. At least he wouldn't be hogging the living room all the time."

"That could be arranged."

I snicker as Belladonna hands me a glass. Witchcraft is the solution to all our problems, even when the problems don't exist yet.

It feels wrong, to come to Belladonna's and *not* work some magic. Even after I landed that book deal, even after Anais snagged Marty and then he snagged his promotion, even after Triss and Elaine moved in together and everyone in town couldn't stop remarking what good friends they were, we still felt that hunger. Magic is its own reward.

Last week, we stopped my exhaust from rattling.

"Maybe we should try our hand at matchmaking again," Elaine suggests. She took a glass of wine in the hand that wasn't holding her wife's. "It was fun last time."

"For us," I mutter.

Not so much for Bob and Gina, or Bob's fiancée. I'm pretty sure I'm the only one who's spoken to Gina since—not for long, because it was hard to watch her cry. Fixing up two random folks from town had seemed like such an interesting idea at the time.

A moment of madness, Bob had said. If only he knew. The madness wasn't his.

"Perhaps we should just...savor this time," Belladonna suggests, pouring her glass last and then pouring herself into her wicker throne.

I lock eyes with Anais over the burgundy. "You feeling okay, Bella?"

"Fine," she sighs. "Don't I seem okay?"

"You seem..."

"Like you already put away a bottle," Anais says. "Seriously, why are you talking like that?"

"We've known each other a long time. We've accomplished a lot together, haven't we? I'm entitled to let my guard down a little among friends. I just want to sit here and enjoy the sunshine, enjoy the company. Enjoy the wine. It's not too much to ask, is it?"

This time, the coven shares the look. Belladonna closes her eyes and hums a few bars to herself. A song I don't recognize, like a lullaby.

Anais mouths, *What the fuck?*

"Ah, leave her alone," I say. "I'm going for a smoke."

They don't try to stop me. Looks like we'll be taking our time with coven business today, so I've got a minute.

I walk a way down the path, fishing my coffin nails out of my jacket. I stop beside the car, check myself in the wing mirror. Teenage folly inspired me to dye my hair black—*Gee, who could I possibly have been emulating?*—and now I'm muddy brown in a way even magic can't seem to fix. I'm starting to gray now too. Maybe I can get away with it. Aren't novelists supposed to be distinguished?

None of us have ever talked about how we're catching up to Belladonna every year. Pretty soon, we'll be gray and grizzled and she'll be as perfect as the day we met her. I find myself wondering what she'll do when we're too old to make it up the hill to the House.

I light up and puff a while in the shade of an elm. I wonder, not for the first time, why Belladonna built her house so goddamn far from town. The place is practically part of the forest. Roots lift slabs, and flowering shrubs poke through the fences, and ivy swarms on *everything*, like it wants this piece of itself back.

Something skitters in the leaves. I jump, cigarette tumbling.

"Fucking rabbits."

At least, I *think* it was a rabbit. It sounded...bigger.

I swat the butt off my jacket, smearing ash down my chest, and swallow a bubble. I start coughing.

I can't stop coughing. I smother a hand over my mouth and

hack until I've thoroughly scratched that itch. By the time I'm done, my chest aches.

"Jesus…" I go to wipe my hand on my jeans. Then I see the blood. "Oh my God. What the fuck?"

I check myself in the car's mirror again. Blood on my lips too. A trickle to the point of my chin. I scrub it off with my jacket sleeve. How…

Dangling from out of my shirt, the rabbit's foot. The white fur has withered gray and shriveled. The flesh has turned paper thin, mummified bones jutting. I snap the cord and hold it the fuck away from me.

I stare up at the house, the veranda. I march back up the path.

I pass Anais on the way. She's shouting into her phone, and I realize I can't remember the last time any of us had to raise our voice. There just isn't enough to be angry at these days.

I shuffle on, and hear Anais shrieking, "Don't you *dare* fucking hang up on me, Marty Gibson!"

Elaine and Triss are standing at the veranda's edge, listening to Anais spitting venom, concern flickering in their eyes, wine forgotten. They stare at the red in my hand, the rotten rabbit's foot in the other. They fish out their own feet and recoil in unison.

No doubt Anais's is the same.

Belladonna is still humming that lullaby. I throw shade on her until she opens her eyes.

There's only one question on my bloody lips. "What the fuck is going on?"

Belladonna sighs. She sets her wine down. "I'm sorry, Loretta. I'm afraid it looks like luck has run out. For all of you."

CHAPTER 2

TRAILER PARK GIRLS

I flash a middle finger salute at the back of the school bus after it unceremoniously dumps us at the entrance to the trailer park. "Assholes."

Mary smirks and shakes her head, sending her dark curls tumbling around her face. "You shouldn't let them get to you, Court."

"I know. I can't help it. It isn't like I want to live here, you know?" Why the bus includes both the poor students from Shady Acres and the rich kids from Rockburn Pass on the same route is beyond me.

Mary's little sister, Grace, comes around my other side. Where Mary is tall and thin, her sister is the opposite. Her round cheeks and reddish-blond hair make her seem younger than her thirteen years. "She's right, Courtney. They always say the same shit anyway. They can't even be bothered to come up with new insults. So, we live in a trailer park? Okay, noted. I mean, move on already."

Shady Acres Mobile Home Park is ringed with dense

forest that might have been beautiful, if not for the tired, old, rusted-out trailers housing the park's inhabitants—mostly folks on retirement or disability. It's the butt of every joke; even the word 'Mobile' is laughable. Most of these trailers have been glued down, complete with their residents, since the 1970s. People only leave Shady Acres for one reason.

They stop breathing.

My little brother lags out of earshot with a couple of boys from the bus. He's still in elementary school, and as such, a colossal pain in my ass. He's far enough behind not to overhear us.

"Hey, do you guys want to grab Dani and meet up at the church later?"

Dani lives in the park too, but after she was caught smoking weed with Rodney Smith, her mom enrolled her in Holy Rock Christian Academy.

Grace's eyes widen. "Me too?"

"Sure," I answer, "we could use another person."

"For what?" Grace and Mary ask in unison.

I shrug, quickening my pace to take the lead. "Guess you'll have to show up to find out, won't you?"

Mary beams down at her little sister, who skips off in the direction of their trailer. "We'll see you later, Courtney."

I freeze as I turn down our street and spot the black Audi convertible sitting in front of the Smiths' trailer. I'd know the car even if its owner weren't leaning against the hood, but I'll be damned if I know what Heather Washburn is doing in Shady Acres.

The Smiths have lived here forever. A pair of sisters who, I'm pretty sure, are older than Meemaw. Sometimes they pay me to walk their dog or pick up groceries from the Piggly Wiggly. Their great-nephew, Rodney stays with them on and off, and it dawns on me what Heather's doing here. She's here to buy weed from Rodney.

Heather wrinkles her nose and sniffs the air. "Eww, gross. Do you smell that, Mikayla?" she asks her clone, sitting in the passenger's seat.

They look interchangeable—dark hair, skin airbrushed and fake-tanned to perfection, French manicured nails. All that money and beauty, and they still need to make people feel like shit.

"Yeah," Mikayla answers. "Smells like garbage."

"Like trailer trash, you mean," Heather says, and they both laugh like it's the first time either of them have heard the joke.

I try to move wide past them, but Heather steps into my path. "Oh, no, it's not garbage, it's just Courtney!" She puts her face close to mine and sniffs. She smells expensive. "You stink, trailer trash."

I know better than to take her bait, but she also knows all the right buttons to push. It's bad enough I have to deal with her bullshit at school, but here? I complain about the trailer park, but it's home, and if a girl isn't safe on her own turf, where is she safe? Heather's presence here is too much. I shove her out of my face and sidestep away.

"Hey!" she shouts, regaining her balance. She shoulders me hard, causing me to fall back against the hood, the same place she was standing moments before.

Mikayla gasps. "Oh. My. God. She touched your car. You're going to have to get it washed now. It's got her germs all over it."

Heather smiles, cruelty spreading across her perfect features. "Courtney Fowler, did you just rub your nasty stink all over my car? This car is worth more than your fucking house."

"Get the fuck away from me, Heather." I try stepping to the side again, but she positions her body directly into my path.

I glance around; I don't see Freddie yet. He's probably distracted with some of his friends. If I run, I could probably get to the trailer before Heather caught me, if she bothered to follow.

I'm still weighing my options when her fist slams into my

stomach and I double over. White-hot pain shoots through my head as she grabs a fist full of my hair and forces my face down to her car.

"Lick it clean," she says.

"What?" Humiliation burns my cheeks.

"You heard me. I said to fucking *lick it clean*."

Mikayla is fumbling inside the car. "Wait, let me get my camera!"

I jerk my head, trying to pull free, to run, but Heather wraps her fist tighter in my hair. I can hear hair ripping out of my scalp. Photos, videos of me licking her car will be all over social media within the hour. I struggle against her, but her grip is tight. The heat radiating off the car warms my cheeks.

"Hey!" Heather and I turn at the same time and see Freddie and two of his pals from the bus charging toward us. He grabs a rock and chucks it at the Audi. "Get off my sister!"

Heather screams. "You fucking brat! I'm going to kill you!"

She lets go of my hair and starts for Freddie. She almost reaches him when the trailer door screeches open and Nancy Smith steps out onto her carport.

"YOUNG LADY!" her voice booms, louder than it should be for a woman her size. "I would advise you not to harm the little boy. I'm sure the police would not take it kindly."

Freddie drops the rock he's aiming at the Audi.

"But," Heather says, "he attacked my car!"

"As a witness, all I saw was *you* attacking a little boy," Nancy says. "And when the police search your car, I'm certain they'll be interested in those little dime bags you think you're hiding in the dashboard."

Heather's face twists in rage. "We're not done," she spits at me, before climbing in her car, slamming the door, and leaving us in her dust.

I turn to Nancy Smith, my guardian angel. "Thank you."

She nods once and goes back inside her trailer.

"Thanks, Freddie," I say, and I can't hide the weariness in my voice. "Come on. Meemaw's gonna be pissed if we make her late for Bingo."

When I get to our trailer, Meemaw's station wagon is already in the driveway. Beside it sits an ancient, powder-blue Volkswagen Beetle that hasn't been on the road since I was little. It's no Audi, but one day, when I save enough money, I'll get it running again.

My legs are still shaking as I dump my textbooks on the bed and grab the box shoved all the way in the back of my closet. I pull out the book, the one I swiped from the old Mason place. Any doubt left in my mind has faded—Heather's presence at Shady Acres made sure of that. I need to protect myself, and something in here might be able to show me how.

I stuff the book into my backpack and set off for the woods, my cheeks still burning with anger and shame.

The forest around Shady Acres is equal parts dump and hideout, depending on who you ask. About a mile out, there's an abandoned factory, still partially intact, but we know not to go there; Meemaw says that's where the meth heads hang out. Instead, Mary, Dani and I found our own spot in the forest.

Past the broken asphalt of what used to be the factory parking lot, we'd stumbled upon a path between three large pines that led to a broken picnic table. Beyond that, we'd discovered ruins—years of abandonment turned into little more than piles of rubble—where forgotten houses once stood. Meemaw told me there was once a mine, and a small settlement of miners had lived in the village. There was a series of accidents, and when the mine closed, the village died out. Shady Acres is built on its grave.

In the center of the ruins is the most intact structure, made mostly of stone. Three partial walls still stand, with a wrought iron crucifix hanging over what might once have been a pulpit. In faded, blue spray paint beneath the crucifix is the number 666, along with a sloppy pentagram.

This is our place. Our church.

The first to arrive, I pull supplies out of my backpack and spread one of Meemaw's old tablecloths over the moss carpeting the crumbling stone floor. An angry chipmunk chirps and sends me sprawling flat on my ass before it vanishes behind the stone wall.

"Getting started already, are we?"

Even if I didn't know the sound of Dani's voice better than my own, the overpowering smell of cigarette smoke would have given her away.

"I invited Grace," I say, turning and taking her in.

She's wearing a pair of jeans cut off too short and a half-tucked flannel shirt. Each strand of her messy bob is meticulously arranged to be out of place, an ordered chaos held together by mousse and Aqua Net. She wears too much eyeliner and a pair of men's combat boots she bought at the Salvation Army. She's been my best friend since the second grade, when she put glue in Heather Washburn's hair for starting a rumor that I had head lice.

"Yeah. I heard her squee from across the park." She pulls a pack of menthols from her pocket and offers me one. I shake my head. I'd tried once but hated the way they made my throat close up. Like I was choking. She shrugs and tucks the pack back into the front pocket of her flannel. "You brought the book?"

I rummage around my backpack and pull out the leather-bound tome, placing it in her waiting hand. It's the oldest-looking book I've ever seen.

She narrows her eyes and flips it open, skimming the first few pages. "Book of Shadows... Most of these are bullshit, but

whatever." She hands it back to me.

"How do you know they're bullshit?"

"I've tried a couple," she says. It's news to me. "*Spells for the Solitary Witch* and all that, but none of the shit in them ever worked. It's just a gimmick to sell books."

"Couldn't hurt to try," I say.

The truth is, I'm nervous. I don't really believe in God or the Devil, but if God *is* real, and we practice witchcraft in what used to be *his house*... Well, that might be a sin worthy of eternal damnation.

I open my mouth to tell Dani about my encounter with Heather. My cheeks burn. I don't want to live through that humiliation again, even in words, so I swallow them back. Telling her would almost be as bad as if she witnessed it, and I don't want her to see me like that.

Dani takes a long drag from her cigarette, then wraps her arms around herself. Did I imagine a shiver? It was early September, and the evenings still lacked an autumn chill.

"You okay?" I ask.

"Yeah. Just...this place. All the people who ever lived here are dead. People used to sit here and pray. There are people buried here, in the churchyard. Does it ever creep you out? That kinda shit puts energy into the world."

"Like ghosts?" I ask.

She gives a noncommittal shrug. "Ghosts, Jesus, whatever."

I want to ask more. I want to know what she thinks and feels about everything, so I can think and feel it all too, but Mary and Grace's heavy steps crunch across the detritus littering the forest floor, bringing our conversation to an end.

"Oh my GOD, this place is amazing!" Grace says, running a hand over the ruined stone wall of the church.

Mary rolls her eyes, but she's smiling at her sister. "Dude, act like you've been somewhere before, okay?"

"Sorry. It's just...I've never seen anything like it before. How old is this place?"

Dani shrugs. "At least a hundred years, probably more."

"More," I answer. "The mines operated back in the seventeen and eighteen hundreds. There was an ironworks and everything. It closed down in the late eighteen hundreds."

"How'd you know all that?" Grace asks, with a furrowed brow.

I look up at Dani, then the others. "I wrote about it in my history report for Mr. Hensley last year."

Grace bites her lip, staring at me. It's pretty obvious she has something else to say.

"What?" I ask.

"I...I got a C-minus in History, and Mom and Dad are pissed. Do you think you might tutor me sometime?"

"Yeah. I can do that."

Dani reaches down and ruffles her fingers through my hair. I hate when she does it, but I love when she does it. "My little nerd."

I hope the muss of hair in my face hides the fact that I'm blushing.

"What's that?" Mary asks, reaching for the book.

"This..." I pause for dramatic effect. "...is the reason we're here today. This book has spells, charms, recipes for talismans, and all kinds of stuff. I thought we might try something out."

Grace stops dancing around the ruins and stares wide-eyed at the book. "Witchcraft? But that's evil. You'll have to sign the Devil's book in blood!"

Mary sighs. "For Christ's sake, Grace, it's fake. It's just something to do. A bunch of hocus pocus."

I lift the book, showing off the cracked leather cover. "It isn't fake. I got this from a real witch."

"Bullshit," Mary says.

The color drains from Grace's face. "How do you know a real witch?"

"You know my meemaw cleans houses, right? I wanted to make some extra cash to fix my car, so she gave me the biggest house because going up and down all those stairs is murder on her knees. Anyway, the lady that lives there is a witch. I saw it with my own eyes. She had all kinds of weird shit."

Dani takes the book from my hands and opens the cover. I almost protest, but the words die on my lips. She runs a finger along the vellum page. "It's old. It's even in funny English."

"If it was real, wouldn't it be written in Latin or something?" Mary asks.

I reach into my bag and pull out the candles, positioning them in the four corners of the tablecloth-covered stone. "There isn't anything special about Latin that makes it more magical than any other language. It's just words." I try to align the candles perfectly, but the stone isn't even, so the northeast corner is a little wonky.

"What are we going to do?" Dani asks, placing the book on the altar.

"You're going to light these candles, and then we're going to find something in the book to test out," I answer. "Something simple to start."

Grace takes a step back. "I don't think this is a good idea."

Dani winks at me, then turns and shakes a cigarette loose. "Hey, Grace, want a smoke?"

Every bit of resistance fades from Grace's features. Dani's a genius. She knows Grace will do what we ask, even if she's afraid, because she wants to fit in. A small, violent shock of jealousy explodes within me when Dani places an arm around Grace's shoulder, as though they've been friends forever.

I can't help but wonder if Dani has always been this good at manipulating people, and I've just never noticed before.

CHAPTER 3

WITHERING HEARTS

The waiting room stinks of antiseptic and I need a fucking cigarette.

There's three other people in the oncology department. Two of them are twice my age and the other is as jaundiced as a lemon. I don't belong here. I don't *want* to belong here.

But this is me now. The appointments have started. Scans, biopsies, consultations. I know the steps to this dance. I've waltzed this way before and my bodice is too tight. I feel like I'm breathing through a clenched fist, like my lungs are half-filled with fluid. Red mists from my mouth with every wheeze.

My fingers curl tight on the handkerchief, just in case.

Doctor Patel's door pops open. She leans through the gap and says, "Loretta Dandridge."

She reaches for my hand and makes me slip the handkerchief into my other palm to shake. My grip feels loose. That seems to be a running theme right now.

We take seats in her office like that time we went for coffee, after we'd won the first time. She's exactly as I remember—pressed, white blouse and thick, black hair, a silver chain in her

neckline that probably isn't a rabbit's foot. The crow's feet have deepened around her almond-shaped eyes, and she looks like she smiles even less now. I click to the signed copy of *Withering Hearts* on her bookshelf, side-by-side with her leather-bound perfect collections of medical texts. I don't know if she ever read it, if she twined fingers with the character I based on her and had a good laugh over the in-jokes we'd shared during my miraculous recovery.

She was never a friend. An ally, at best. She never knew what really happened that summer all those years ago, when we hexed the shit out of my cancer.

I wonder if she kept the book or found it in a box somewhere when my name reappeared on her schedule. It's flattering to think it's been there the whole time.

"How have you been, Loretta?"

"Better."

"When did you first start to notice something was wrong."

"A week ago."

Her eyebrows levitate from under the rim of her glasses. Yes, everyone's very surprised at how quickly I've slid back down the rabbit hole. Everyone except Belladonna, who's acting like this was all part of the plan since that day she asked me if I believed in magic, and who isn't returning my calls.

"Well, I've reviewed the file. I'm afraid it isn't good news."

"I already knew that. I have cancer. Again."

I scratch at my pockets, trying to unearth a cigarette. I left the box in my car because I knew what would happen if I brought them inside.

"I've reviewed your options based on the probability of success and, at this stage, I can't recommend chemotherapy. Given the position of the masses I've seen, surgery wouldn't seem a viable option either."

"So, what does that leave me?"

"We need to look at your pain management, most likely a

course of anti-inflammatories. I know you live alone, but it would be helpful if you could have a social support structure in place. Are you still in touch with those women from your earlier appointments? Anais and...Triss and Elaine, was it?"

I'm still Tetrising her words into place in my head as she starts to fan-spread pamphlets for charity organizations and support groups who can "help to meet my needs". Maybe it's the way I have to force my lungs to work now or the way this still all feels like a nightmare, but it takes me a while to fill a line.

Then the stack crashes down.

"This is palliative care," I grunt. Doctor Patel falls silent. "Why are we talking about palliative care? It's been a week."

"Since the onset of major symptoms but...this has obviously been advancing for quite some time, Loretta. I know it's not what you wanted to hear—"

I start laughing. Can't help myself. She's just told me I'm dying and there's nothing she or I can do about it, but I'm struck by the absurdity of an oncologist who gets to regularly tell people what they want to hear.

Maybe there's a novel in that.

Unfortunately, I can't hold back the laughter and I can't hold back the coughing that follows. I hack until I retch into my handkerchief. My mouth is full of red slime, and I remember the terror of drowning in my own bodily fluids that I thought I'd finally put behind me for good.

Doctor Patel passes me her wastepaper basket and I drop the hankie in it with a wet splat. She'll need to have it burned and her office sanitized. I try not to be ashamed. I am the greatest victim of my body's betrayal. Even so, I apologize.

"You don't need to be sorry, Loretta. This isn't your fault."

She reaches across the table and squeezes my hand. Unfortunately, we both know it's a platitude. She can see the nicotine stains on my fingers, same as she saw them last time.

And we both know that, even if she's willing to overlook

them, my insurance company won't be.

"Is that it?" I ask. "Nothing else we can do?"

"Nothing your insurance will cover."

"Maybe you can look into other options anyway. I might be able to work something out."

"The price of an experimental treatment, the possibility of success, with your condition at this stage…"

"Please." I hate the desperation in my voice and the pity in her eyes. It's the furthest from Belladonna's batting eyelashes and curled lips I could have fallen. "Look into it for me. What's the harm, right?"

She purses her lips, then says something that makes me feel like I've misjudged our relationship, because doctors don't say things like that—only friends do.

"Hope can be harmful."

"Please," I say again, and rise from my seat. There's nothing else left to say.

"You're not wearing your rabbit's foot anymore," she says. I forgot we talked about it once before. Apparently, she didn't forget.

"I don't need luck," I whisper. "I need a fucking miracle."

Out in the car, I realize how ill-prepared I am for this. I have money, a house, possessions. That used to mean something, before all this, but how long will they last when the bills begin to pile up? I have an estate and intellectual property, life insurance, and there'll be posthumous royalties, none of which will do me any good.

I could ask Anais and Elaine and Triss for help, but…

They're my coven. We meet up once a week to work magic. Are we still friends? We were before. But this time, no one was there to hold my hand in the waiting room. No one was there to remind me that we were bad ass witches, and we were going to make that cancer wish it had never existed.

Anais can't seem to stop fighting with Marty. Elaine and Triss have been hiding from us since Belladonna's veranda. Forget Belladonna. There's no one I can call.

I clutch my phone so tight my knuckles go white as I scroll through my contacts and realize there's *still* no one I can call.

Except my publisher.

"Loretta! How's things, girl?"

At least someone sounds happy to hear from me. Of course, that's going to change.

"I need an advance."

Pregnant pause. *"An advance on what?"*

"On a new book. A sequel to *Withering Hearts.*"

Seeing Doctor Patel again has me curious to know how her character might have changed in the decade since. I never dreamed of doing a continuation—it should have been one and done—but I'm desperate. In every conceivable way.

"Loretta, have you spoken to—"

"You're the first person I've spoken to. Come on, Patty. You know I'm good for it. I'm still selling. I get letters about *Hearts.* People want a sequel."

"Maybe..." Her voice is a non-committal thread and my life dangles from it. *"Arthur's been trying to get in touch with you all week. He got a call from someone at Amazon. They're thinking of optioning* Letters from the Lost Days *for an original series."*

I smother a groan and try not to cough because I don't have another handkerchief. Plus, I don't want Patty to realize I might not be able to make good on any advance she extends me.

Letters was always my problem child. I hated every page of it when I wrote it, and I hated every sentence when I edited. But it was the book we published, as a coven. It was the first thing I ever wanted for myself, and it took me over a year to firm my ovaries

enough to ask them if we could work the spell. A little taste of success.

It had snowballed from there. I only really started to love the job once the pressure was off.

Still, my luck must be holding out if somebody's still interested.

"Okay. Who do I need to talk to?"

"You don't need to talk to anyone. Arthur's going ahead with the project. He's asked L.T. Lancer to write the screenplay."

"He asked Lewis to write a screenplay for my fucking book?"

"It's the company's book, Loretta. Remember?"

Something in her tone reminds me of the way Belladonna spoke to me, on the veranda last week.

I'm afraid it looks like luck has run out.

Of course. Because I was fresh off the boat and I didn't read the small print and, frankly, I was glad to see the back of *Letters* anyway. I signed on for an advance, for royalties, and signed away the property in the process. Which means I don't stand to make a penny from this.

"I'll call you back."

"Loretta—"

Smart phones don't slam but I slam this one anyway, right off the dashboard. Pieces of the screen plink against the windshield like rain.

"Fuck," I growl, and before I can stop myself, I'm pounding on the steering wheel with my red, red hands, horn bleating under my abuse. "Fuck, fuck, fuck!"

I seize the rearview in white knuckles and twist it, like snapping a rabbit's neck. I hate when people watch me cry. Then I sag in the driver's seat and squeeze my eyes shut.

"Fuck..."

CHAPTER 4

HONEYSUCKLE FULL OF POISON

"Thanks for letting me stay the night," Dani says, looking through the large stack of CDs on the rack that once belonged to my mom. Still belongs to her, I suppose, not that Teeny bothers coming around much anymore. Her collection is expansive, ranging from classic rock to grunge to emo, and more.

"No problem. You know you're always welcome."

She's been staying at my house more often since her mom started dating Skeezy Skeet. I'm not sure what his real name is, everyone's always called him Skeet. We gave him the nickname *Skeezy* because everything about him skeeves us out—the greased-back hair, the shirt unbuttoned to expose too much chest hair, and the smell like he's gone swimming in a vat of cheap cologne. He's unemployed and holding out for a management position, so he says. I think he's looking for a free ride. So does Dani.

Dani grabs Hole's *Celebrity Skin* and pops it into the ancient boombox on my nightstand. She thinks they're my favorite band since Teeny named me after Courtney Love. The truth is, I think they suck, but I'll never tell Dani that.

She flashes a hesitant smile. It's unlike her to show gratitude or vulnerability. Our friendship feels unbalanced at times, and though a tinge of guilt creeps over me, it's damn good to know she needs me as much as I need her.

"Can I see the book?"

I nod and dig it out of my backpack, a faded, navy-blue Jansport covered in iron-on patches.

She opens the book, studying the title page. "Did you really mean what you said?" she asks, not making eye contact.

"About what?"

"About the lady. The witch? Were you for real, or just talking shit to show off for Mary and Grace?"

"She had some really creepy shit in her house, which is huge, by the way." It was hard to explain the way my skin broke into goosebumps when I saw the book, the way I felt like someone was watching me the whole time I was there. The smell, like a wet dog or something, that lingered in the rooms, despite my scrubbing. "And not Halloween creepy, either. It was like some shrunken heads kinda stuff. All kinds of herbs hanging everywhere. Big Goya prints on the walls. I mean, seriously freaky."

I'm not sure why, but seeing Dani with the book gives me a sense of unease. Like déjà vu for something that hasn't happened yet.

"If you thought she was a real witch, why'd you take the book? She'll notice it missing, and know you took it. For someone so smart, you didn't think it through." She flips a few pages in. "Besides, the spell we tried didn't work. We all saw it. Nothing happened. It's not real."

The springs of my ancient, white daybed squeal in protest as I sit beside her. "I took it because it felt right. It was just lying there, like it was left for me to find." Heat rises to my cheeks. I'm not making sense. "It didn't feel like stealing, more like finding something I lost."

I wait for her to laugh or tell me I'm being ridiculous, but she just nods.

"It's pretty cool. But if she is a real witch, and it is a real book, I don't get why it didn't work."

"How do you know it didn't? All we did was cast a circle of protection. How can you tell if that worked?"

The book is open to the spell we cast in the woods. We picked that one because it was the easiest. It didn't require any special items to cast. That's what I had told the others, anyway. The real reason, the one I didn't say aloud, was that I wanted protection from Heather. I knew she wouldn't let what Freddie had done go, and I knew she'd eventually take it out on me.

"I don't know. I guess I just expected to feel something." Her tone betrays her disappointment, and I know without a doubt that she wants to believe.

"I think I did."

She scoots closer to me on the bed. "What did you feel?"

"I don't know." I pause for the right words. *Less afraid.* "Powerful?"

"Do you think we could really use this to do stuff? Like, not lame shit like protection, but...you know, make things happen?" Her leg presses against mine, and my flesh lights up like it's on fire.

I swallow hard and look at the floor, the wall, anywhere but at Dani. "What kind of things?"

"Get rid of Skeet, for one thing. You could bring Teeny back and get her clean and have a real mom for once."

"I don't need her." I pull my leg away and stand, ejecting *Celebrity Skin.* "I like it just fine here with Meemaw and Freddie. I hate Courtney Love, and I fucking hate Teeny."

"So..." Dani starts.

"So what?" I ask, slamming the CD back into its case. I grab *Jagged Little Pill* and pop it into the player.

"So, then, let's do something about it," she says, waving the book at me. "Let's look in here and see what's possible."

There's a knock at the door and Meemaw's face appears in the cracked doorway. "Dinner's just about ready, ladies. Why don't you go get washed up and set the table for us?"

"Of course, Mrs. Fowler," Dani replies, in her sweetest voice. I've come to recognize it as her talking-to-adults voice. She shoves the book under my pillow and we head to the kitchen.

"How's your momma, Danielle?" Meemaw asks as we fold paper napkins into triangles. "She still workin' at the sewing plant?"

"She's okay. She got a promotion, so she's been working more overtime, but she's happy about it." She unfolds and refolds the same napkin twice. "Courtney said you got her work cleaning houses?"

"Sure did. You interested in some work too?"

"Maybe. She said you sent her to a witch's house." Dani grimaces in pain as I grind the heel of my Converse into the top of her foot.

Meemaw chuckles. "She's what you might call eccentric, but she ain't a witch. People in this town like to talk, that's all. Can't stand a woman living alone and doin' alright by herself." She places a large platter of garlic bread beside the chipped bowl of spaghetti on the table. "Why don't you call Freddie in for dinner? There are some things we need to discuss."

"I ain't gonna beat around the bush," Meemaw says, looking first at Freddie, then me.

Whatever she's going to tell us, I know I'm not going to like. I pick at a loose thread hanging from the faded tablecloth.

"Your momma called today. She's coming home. She'll be staying with us for a while."

My heart sinks. If Teeny is coming to stay here, it means she's using again and trying to get clean, or she's gotten in legal or money trouble, or all of the above.

"When?" I ask, barely able to choke out the word.

"She'll be here this weekend. She'll be sleeping on the couch."

I nod and push my chair back. Any appetite I had is gone, replaced with a feeling like a rock in the pit of my stomach. Teeny coming home is never good for any of us.

My eyes flicker to Freddie's seat. He's smiling. He's still too young to understand Momma's problem, and the whispers of *junkie* haven't reached his ears yet.

I don't remember to excuse myself before leaving the kitchen.

Dani mutters apologies and follows me to my room, closing the door behind her.

Teeny has always stormed in and out of our lives like a hurricane. I've asked Meemaw why she welcomes her back every single time, and I always get the same answer, some variation of: *Your mother has problems. She can't help the way she is. She's troubled.*

I've never been able to do anything about it. Until now. It can't be a coincidence that the book has found me just when I need it.

I fling back the quilt and pillow. "Okay. Let's see what we can do."

CHAPTER 5

The Fix

My publisher puts out a press release, telling everyone that I'm "taking some time away". They cancel my conference appearances and Zoom interviews and email me a two hundred-page PDF of their contractual responsibilities to my next of kin in the event of my death.

When asked for a name, I write the only one I can think of, even if I haven't seen her in twenty years.

Their website lights up with news about the Amazon show. *For fans of Loretta Dandridge.* That's the only time my name appears.

I'm hungover when Anais calls. I answer the phone on the first ring. Might seem desperate but, honestly, I'm past caring. The only living creature I've spoken to since my appointment is a cat that doesn't even belong to me.

"It's good to hear your voice, Anais," I sigh, once she's through ranting about her husband.

"You drunk, Lori?"

"Post-drunk. Think I'm out of booze."

"Why don't you come around here? I'm tired of drinking alone."

If there'd been a hand attached to that invitation, I'd have taken it off at the wrist. I crawl into my car, swatting pieces of my cell phone off the seat, and drive like a moron to Anais's home. The way my luck's going, I should get pulled over or drive into a ditch.

My cabin's a small place. Quaint, I like to call it. Anais prefers to emasculate me by calling it cute. It has a desk, a bed, a shower with fucking amazing water pressure and occasional squirrels in the garden. I don't need more than that.

Anais's place isn't cute. It's a fortress of oak siding built into the side of the hill, like a giant wearing trees as camouflage. Three floors, a pool, matching His & Hers garages with matching His & Hers cars parked in them. Magic has never found the limits of her ambition like it has mine, Triss and Elaine's.

I park crooked in the driveway and stagger to the front door in sweats and a track top with my blood on the sleeve. Anais isn't waiting for me with a bottle and a hug when I arrive, so I bang on the door like a repo man, come to get the friendship I think I'm owed.

I'm dying. Sitting at home with only the neighbor's cat for company has made me wonder what I've done wrong. Have I been such a bad person that I deserve to die alone?

Only, that's not the point, is it? Maybe I haven't been a bad person, but I haven't exactly been a *good* person either. What have I ever done to help anyone but myself? What reason have I given anyone else to care?

Anais's call feels like my last chance. The possibility of redemption. And she isn't even the one who opens the door.

"Morning, Loretta," Marty says, waving me into the house.

"Is it morning? I've been sleeping into the afternoon lately. What even is time?"

"Are you...alright? You don't look well."

I hesitate, press my bloody sleeve against my flank. "Anais hasn't told you?"

"Anais hasn't told me a lot of things, apparently."

He studies me for a few long moments, and I tap out after the first second. My eyes pass to the younger, happier Marty who was the King to Anais's Prom Queen in the photograph on the wall. She has the tiara perched in her frizzy hair, grinning the biggest, bucktooth grin, freckled all over and a look of vicious triumph in her eyes. No one saw that coming. Would you be surprised if I told you we'd used magic?

"Did you know?" he asks me, snapping me from the comfort of past victories.

"Know what?"

"About Anais?"

"About Anais *what?*"

He rolls his eyes. Apparently, I've failed that pop quiz. "I suppose I shouldn't have expected an honest answer from one of her friends," he says, and storms off out of the house without saying goodbye.

"Great talk, Marty."

I find Anais in the kitchen. We "fixed" her frizzy hair and her buck teeth and her freckles a long time ago. Now she looks like someone who'd have made Prom Queen without magic. Like the kind of girls we called bitches in high school, and we could never decide if we hated them because we had it figured out, or if we were jealous because we thought they did.

Turned out none of us had it figured out back then. We were all fuckups.

Even wearing pajamas and bed hair, she looks amazing. My appearance is the one thing I never wasted a spell on, but pretty soon after she started dating Marty, started going to the parties and the business lunches, she started talking about all the things she hated about herself. And, because we were her friends and because we were idiots, we changed her instead of sticking up for her.

She pours me a glass. A very full glass. Her own is already full, and it probably isn't the first of the day.

"What's up with Marty?" I ask.

"He's a dick, that's what."

"Right. Where was he going? He didn't look happy."

"Who cares. That's not why I called you over. I think I figured it out."

"Figured what out?"

"Why the magic isn't working."

I've read the stages of grief. I've flown through a couple of signposts on that road already. I'm ready to start bargaining. "Okay, why?"

The only person I expected to know the truth was Belladonna and she hasn't spoken to us since the day our rabbit's feet shriveled. The day the luck ran out. I'm desperate for a revelation. Whatever Anais is selling, I need her to shut up and take my money.

"We're not doing real magic. Think about it. Every week we meet up and we put together some weak-sauce love potion or hex some guy who cuts in line at the donut shop or fix your fucking car. That's not why we became witches, Lori. We became witches because this world was fucking us, and we wanted to fuck it back. When was the last time we did something that really mattered?"

"It's been a long while, I guess."

"So, we need to get Triss and Elaine and cast a *real* spell, like we used to." She lowers her voice, lays a hand gently on mine, meets my eyes with the kind of intensity I associate with kissing. "And I think I know what kind of spell we need."

I nod and blink back tears. This whole time, I thought none of them cared. I thought they'd forgotten about me in among all

their own issues. But my friend is going to come through for me, just like she always has.

We're going to bring the magic back and get me through this together, like we did before. I could weep.

"When was the last time we tried a death hex?"

"A *what?*"

Shock dries up those tears before they come. The fantasy I was living in just a second ago has collided with reality and I can't see where all the pieces went.

Fuck, I'm such an idiot.

"I mean it, Lori. We want to do serious magic, ain't no magic more serious than that."

"Yeah, you're telling me."

I drain half my glass in a single swallow. We haven't used that magic since we were teenagers and I was happier when the details were hazy, when I didn't have to think about the fact that we *killed* people.

People who deserved it? Yeah, we convinced ourselves of that. Maybe we believed it too. Except we'll never know for sure because you can't turn a life around once it's ended.

"Who were you thinking of killing?" I ask bitterly, biting back the urge to tell her just to wait a little while, because pretty soon I'll give her all the death she can handle. "I mean, Triss's dad was a wife-beating piece of shit who probably would have killed her if we'd let him. Brad locked Elaine in the trunk of his car and threatened to slit her throat. Do you even know anyone like that anymore?"

"There are plenty of people out there who deserve to die, Lori."

I want to ask her if I'm one of them, but I don't. Instead, I wait for her to suggest what she's been waiting to suggest since I walked in the door. Who is it that she needs my help to murder?

"Marty. I want to kill Marty."

She must see, from the look on my face, that I can't believe what she's suggesting. She and Marty have been perfect for over twenty years. I was one of three bridesmaids at their wedding. I made a speech about their relationship being "some kind of magic" and everyone laughed but only four of us got the joke.

And that's when it hits me. Their relationship *was* some kind of magic. And the magic has run out.

"Alright, what the fuck is going on?"

"I can't keep him in line anymore. He wants a divorce. He's going to take everything and put me out on the street."

"How? You've been married nearly twenty years. You've got rights."

"I signed a prenup."

"So what? That's only important if..."

Her cheeks go as deep red as the wine we're drinking and suddenly I realize how little I know about my best friend.

"Oh my *god*, are you kidding me? You were *cheating* on him too? What the hell, Anais?"

"Don't judge me. Do you think this life is easy? There are so many expectations and I just...I just wanted something uncomplicated."

"You *hexed* him in love with you. And then, what? Hexed him again so he didn't realize you were stepping out on him? Jesus."

"See? This is exactly what I was talking about. Expectations. 'Oh, you and Marty are *so* perfect for each other, Anais. What a beautiful home you have. How do you do it? What's your secret?' I don't get to complain, Lori. It ruins this image everyone has of us. Do you know how many of the pictures on these fucking walls I'm *actually* smiling in?"

I don't respond because I already know the answer. Even the Prom Queen photo has a strain to it.

There's always been anger in Anais, but magic has made her life easier and she's never learned to deal. Without the magic,

she's back to coping the way she used to when she was a kid.

Badly.

"You've got to help me get out of this, Lori. Please. You're my friend."

I think she wants to grasp my fingers, but she seizes my wrist instead, and her fingernails cut through my skin. The desperation in her eyes is frightening. She stands to lose everything unless we can turn this around quickly and the quickest way is to get rid of Marty.

Suddenly, I understand why Doctor Patel told me that hope can be dangerous.

"That doesn't mean I just give you what you want. Maybe you should just...talk to Marty. Work something out."

Her pleading eyes turn hard and cold. "Work what out? He won't forgive me. He wants me gone. Well, two can play at that game. I know what I'm going to do. I'm going to buy him tickets to his precious fucking game. A little peace offering. The moment he's out of town, we cast the spell. He dies on the freeway somewhere, far away from here, and the problem is solved."

"He's not a bad guy, Anais. He's—"

"Not a bad guy? Are you fucking joking? He's going to take *everything* from me. How does that make him 'not a bad guy?'"

I can't think of what to say. I just stand from my stool at the breakfast bar. Her fingernails have left red grooves all around my forearm.

She composes herself enough to drink some more. "Either you help me, or I'll find someone who will."

"How are you going to—"

"That's none of your fucking business, Lori. If you're out, you're out."

It's one of the hardest things I've ever had to say, because Anais is my friend—best, for a lot of years—but I can't condone this. I wish the magic would come back and fix her marriage and smite my cancer, but it's not coming back, which means it's up to us. Fix what can be fixed. Accept what can't.

I'm going to die. But I'm not going to die with an innocent man's blood on my hands.

"I'm out," I say, and I leave.

I sit in the car for about ten minutes before I drive away. My life is crumbling around me and I'm running out of pieces to cling to.

Before I know it, I'm on the road to Triss and Elaine's place.

CHAPTER 6

THREE BLIND MICE

LORETTA

We stand on the deck out back and stare into the trees. The cigarette slowly dwindles between my fingertips. The smoke's silk has turned to sandpaper and sawdust in my throat and I can hardly stand more than a couple of drags.

It pisses me off that I keep coming back to them, after everything they've cost me.

Triss leans on the rail beside me, a cigarette drooping between her full lips. She restrains her braids with a butterfly clip Elaine bought her for their anniversary one year, nestled to the back of her head. Her dark skin holds the shimmer of the day's dying light. Men's shirts, jeans and logging boots to her wife's summer dresses and slingbacks.

I've always admired her practicality. Unlike Anais and Elaine and me, her spells weren't about being noticed. She just wanted to be left alone. Her grandaddy was a mining foreman, brought in from Pennsylvania during the 60s. He could have gone home when they shut the pits up, but he refused. They'd put him out of the job too and besides, the place was his home now. Didn't matter how many times they broke his windows or scorched his lawn or sprayed that word on his front door.

I reckon Triss must have inherited that stubborn streak from him. Except she had magic on her side, so the angry glares turned to "How do you do, ma'am", and the turds on the doorstep turned to bake sale flyers.

I can hear Elaine singing in the kitchen, hear birds twittering in the high branches, hear my lungs crackling only a little, and I don't want the peace I feel to end. But I know I've borrowed this moment and the bill is coming due.

"Anais wants to kill Marty," I tell Triss, flicking ash into the weeds under the deck.

"Not surprised. He wants a divorce."

"You knew already?" It's a stupid question, and I realize it as the words are halfway gone. Of course she knew. Anais needs her coven to cast a spell like that.

"Marty's not a bad guy."

"Maybe not. But you don't cross one of ours."

I grunt. I can hear how noncommittal it sounds. Except I can't shake the feeling that Anais isn't the one being crossed. She used magic to put herself in Marty's bed, and to put his grandmother's ring on her finger. The only reason she stands to lose everything is because she violated a prenup she never even needed to sign.

Does he deserve to die for wanting out of what *we* did to him?

I ask Triss that same question.

She glares at me. "Love isn't a feeling, Lori. It's a choice. Marty's been coasting for years, even with a spell on him. Why do you think Anais went elsewhere? They've been married near twenty years. If he cared about her at all, he'd show it, right?"

"I guess."

I don't like the idea, but there's a reason for that. If it's true, shouldn't my publisher have grown to love me, love my books, despite the spell? What if they dropped me because I honestly never deserved what I got?

That can't be all twenty years of my life was worth.

"Did you hear someone stole the Book of Shadows?"

That gets my attention. I look around at Triss and I'm lucky I don't have the cigarette in my mouth. It would have slipped right out. "No shit? Who took it?"

"Belladonna wouldn't say. She just said it 'found a new home'. Last time I was there, I saw some white trash girl cleaning up the place. Housekeeper's kid, maybe. She probably took it. Trailer park girls get sticky fingers."

"Hey, we started out in that trailer park, remember?"

Some of us never made it out either. I wonder if Triss remembers Christie. I remember her. Remember her lips and her tears and the pain I felt when she didn't look back.

Where is she now? I've started to think about the past a lot. About regrets. She numbers among the greatest of them.

"It's not like I don't get it," Triss says. "When shit's hard, you'll take anything you can get to take the edge off. How's she supposed to know the book's weak without the ritual?"

"She'll figure it out," I mutter. "Or she won't, and she'll spend many happy nights out there in the forest chanting and dancing naked around a bonfire achieving exactly nothing."

I wonder if our lives would have been better or worse if the book had been a dud.

Someone knocks at the front door. The sound of their fist reverberates around the cottage. Triss glances over her shoulder and I catch a glimpse of Elaine's floral-print dress and blond hair flashing in the window as she prances past, on her way to answer.

"So, you spoke to Belladonna?" I ask.

Triss purses her lips. Was she trying to hide it from me? "Not much. I stopped in to ask her about our ward, but she didn't say much. Blew me off, said we didn't have time to worry about it, whatever the hell that means. I went looking for the book, figured I'd do it myself, and it was gone."

"She's not returning any of my calls."

"She's never really been a fan of the phone. Why didn't you go see her?"

I let my eyes fall shut. It's become my answer for so many things recently and I hate it, but...

Because I'm tired.

"Who was at the door, babe?"

I sigh. A moment to gather my thoughts and I've lost her. Not that I, or anyone else, could ever compete with Elaine in her eyes.

The moment stretches out into discomfort. Triss flicks her cigarette into the pile further down the hill and turns to the house.

"Babe?"

Another few seconds is all the grace Triss is willing to give the silence that has taken up residence in her house. She storms in through the back door and I flick my cigarette after hers so I can follow.

Elaine isn't at the front door. She's sitting in the living room with her hands folded in her lap, lips pursed and eyes down. There are three men standing around her. One of them's eyeing a piece of sculpture on the mantle that depicts two women embracing, while another sprawls across the couch with his boots still on.

The third stands behind Elaine, one hand on her shoulder.

"Well, shit," he says, staring right at me. "Loretta Dandridge is here too. Yeah, I guess that figures. Always kind of had that feeling about you, Lori."

"What are you doing in my house, Peej?" Triss demands.

He grins and I suddenly place him. Paul Johannsen, our year in high school. P.J. back then, and a problem to be fixed, because

he seemed to take a girl's lack of interest as a personal challenge. Triss straightened him out with a perception spell.

Only the magic ran out, didn't it?

"Just came around to move that scrap outta your driveway, Triss. Then I thought to myself, why not stop in and be a good neighbor? See if the ladies need any help with anything while we're here?"

"We don't need help. We never needed help. We just want to be left alone."

"I'm pretty sure there are things we can do for you. If you're willing to do a little something for us."

"What the fuck do you want?"

I can hear the growl rising in Triss's throat and I wonder how they can't hear it. How are they not afraid?

"How about putting on a little show for us?" Peej says, and runs his oil-stained hand through Elaine's hair. I see her lips tremble and her hands clench into fists.

Triss takes a step forward. Peej's friend, by the fire, launches the sculpture at her. It hits her full in her face, snaps her head back, then he kicks her so hard in the stomach she knocks photo frames of their wedding day off the wall.

"She ain't so pretty anyway," the other guy says, springing off the couch and seizing me by the elbow. "It'd be better with you. What's say you kiss her for us?"

I open my mouth like I'm going to agree. Instead, I cough in his face. Blood freckles his cheeks and reds his eyes. He recoils like he's going to slap me, and I kick him between the legs.

He slumps back to the couch, gasping. His friend backhands me so hard I almost spin a full circle. It's why I see what's coming, even though he doesn't.

Triss, blood streaming down one side of her face, soaking her shirt, swinging a home run with a bat so new this might be its first pitch. I watch Peej's friend crumpling in slow motion, like his hand knocked something loose in my head. Ear flattening, eye socket deforming, cheek caving, nose bursting, teeth splintering, skull cracking.

He falls through the coffee table where I once drank espresso made from beans Elaine roasted herself. He doesn't try to get up. He's not even breathing anymore.

"Holy shit, lady! You—"

It's all his groin-strained friend can say before Triss brings the hammer down on him too. His neck snaps back like a Pez dispenser and blood sprays from his mouth instead of a pellet. Triss's bare feet streak the cherry wood floor with it.

Peej yanks Elaine out of her seat, toppling the chair over in the process. He backs up against the wall, one hand wrapped around her slim neck. In Triss's eyes, he is already dead. I'm amazed he can't see it yet.

"You piece of shit. You come into *my* house. You touch *my* wife. You're fucking *dead*! You hear me?"

"You think *I'm* dead?" he chuckles. "You just killed two people. It's gonna be old school justice when we come for you. We're gonna string you up."

Triss smiles.

It's the least happy I've ever seen her.

"I'm not finished yet."

Peej doesn't notice the nail file in Elaine's fist until she drives it into his thigh. He roars with pain and lets her go, just long enough that she can escape. His hand seizes her ponytail, but it's too late. Triss is already moving.

The bat crushes his head against the wall. He slithers down, red snail trail streaking the paper, then Triss's bare heel mashes his face to pulp. She stamps him into the floor until he isn't even trying to defend himself.

Then she lifts the bat one more time, like she's bursting watermelons on the beach. She decorates in arterial spray.

I sit on the couch next to a dead man and stare at the wall. I am aware of Triss seizing Elaine in her arms, smoothing hair out of her face and kissing away her tears. The bat has splintered with her ferocity. It has snagged hair from ruined scalps and there is blood.

A lot of blood.

I don't feel time passing but it must, because the next thing I know, Triss is shaking my shoulder.

I wonder how much of my life has passed exactly like that, as I sat completely unaware.

"Lori, help me clean this up."

"Wha—"

"Please! I need to bury these sons of bitches and mop up the blood. I need your help."

I peer up at her and I feel exhaustion in my bones. I want to sleep. I want to sleep forever. But I push myself to my feet and I ignore the flimsiness in my knees and the way my head spins. I need to help Triss. I need to help Elaine. Whatever else is happening right now, they're still my coven. They're still my friends.

And I don't want to die knowing I failed them.

CHAPTER 7

Unforgivable Sins

COURTNEY

It's past midnight on Friday when a loud *thump* and a cry of "Oww, goddamn it!" announces Teeny's arrival. If I were a better daughter, I'd get out of bed to greet her. I'd say hello and pretend to be happy to see her, but she's never done those things for me, and I'm too old for make believe.

I flick on the nightstand lamp. The glow in the dark moon and stars stickers on the ceiling vanish, another relic from when this room was Teeny's.

Dani groans and rubs her eyes. Her head is by my feet. It's the only way we can both fit on the cramped twin-sized mattress. It usually works out fine, besides that one time when she kicked my face in her sleep.

"What is it?" she asks, sitting up. Eyeliner is smudged under her eyes; she didn't bother washing it off before bed. She's wearing a pair of my pajamas patterned with constellations and shooting stars. They look better on her. But then, what doesn't?

"She's here," I answer.

"And?" Dani tugs free a corner of the blanket.

I sigh and fold my arms under my head. "I don't know. I hoped she wouldn't show. Wouldn't have been the first time."

Another thump sounds from the hallway, this time followed by a giggle. My doorknob rattles and eventually turns, and Teeny pokes her head in. "Hey, baby!"

"What do you want?" I don't bother masking the annoyance in my tone.

"That's no way to speak to your mother. I saw your light on. I thought I'd say hi!"

She hangs on the doorframe, the stench of booze and stale cigarettes radiates off her. She's lost at least ten pounds she couldn't afford since the last time I saw her. Her burnt-out, bleached-blond locks are dry and frizzy at the ends, with dark roots peeking through her scalp.

"You're drunk."

She giggles as though I've said something naughty and comes inside, settling herself on the corner of the bed beside me. "Am not! We should catch up. How's school? You're, what, a freshman now?"

"Junior."

"Oh." Her forehead creases and the mask of buzz-fueled happiness slips for a moment.

My own mother can't remember how old I am. Is it the booze that makes her forget, or the lack of giving a shit?

"Is the Washburn girl still giving you trouble?" she asks. "Momma says you and her went at it a few doors down from here."

Dani raises a brow. It was better when she was at the same school. Heather had been afraid of her, and only bothered me when Dani wasn't around. Ever since Dani's mom pulled her out, Heather had declared open season on Courtney Fowler. Not that Teeny cared.

"How do you know about that?" I ask.

"I went to school with her daddy," she says, ignoring my question. "He was a nasty piece of shit too. Celebrated football player, bigot and all-American asshole. I guess the apple don't fall far from the tree." She slurs the last.

The door at the end of the hall creaks open and Meemaw's heavy steps approach. "Christie, you're sleeping on the couch. You leave them girls alone, they need their rest."

Teeny snorts and rolls her eyes. "Alright, Momma."

Meemaw offers an apologetic smile. "Goodnight again, girls. Sweet dreams."

Teeny giggles and starts singing the chorus of the Eurythmics song as Meemaw pulls the door closed behind her.

Dani tugs at my ankle. "You got in a fight with Heather?"

"It wasn't a big deal," I say, but I feel how red my face is.

"What happened?"

"She was being her usual fucking self," I reply.

"Why didn't you tell me?" she asks.

"Because I was embarrassed, okay?"

I'm saved from having to say more as Teeny's voice echoes down the hall, still belting out the slurred chorus, *Sweet dreams are made of these...*

"The only sweet dream she has is happy hour at Mudder's Hole," I grumble.

Dani laughs, and it's that, not Teeny's drunken singing, that fills my ears as I fall back to sleep.

The next morning, I stuff the book in my backpack and shake Dani awake. "Let's go get Mary and Grace."

Dani wipes the sleep from her eyes, which only serves to smear her eyeliner more, and grabs yesterday's clothes.

When I turn, I see a fresh line of bruises high up her arms, shoulders and back. Put there by someone practiced, someone who knew the places they were less likely to be seen. I should ask her about Skeet.

I should beg her to tell someone, but I think about Heather and my own shame, and instead say, "You can borrow something of mine if you want."

She always refuses. My clothes are at least two sizes too large for her and drape off her like tents. She sniffs the armpits of her shirt. "It's fine."

"You really should just leave some of your crap here," I say.

She slips on her shoes, and we head out. Meemaw's already gone for the morning, but Teeny groans from her position on the sofa as the screen door slams shut behind us. She'll be nursing one hell of a hangover when she finally rolls off the couch.

Dani and I set off to Mary and Grace's house. They live on a corner lot in a doublewide, one of the newest—and largest— trailers in the park. Mary told us once that their dad had a job in tech before the company downsized and laid him off. She didn't outright say they'd been rich, but she's the only person I know from Shady Acres who's ever owned an iPhone, so there's that.

Two taps on the window are met by Mary's scowling, half-awake face. It had been our signal since their family moved in two years ago. She nods when I hold up the book. Five minutes later, she and Grace slip onto the redwood deck out back, and we ride our bikes to the church.

"What's so important we can't sleep in?" Mary asks, when we finally arrive, propping our bikes against the ruined walls.

"Sorry," I reply. "I had to get out of that house."

"Is it Freddie or your meemaw giving you a hard time?" she asks.

"Neither," Dani cuts in, before I can answer. "Her momma's back."

Mary cringes, but Grace tilts her head, looking first at Dani, then me. "Isn't that a *good* thing?"

I choke back a laugh. "It ain't when your momma's a junkie."

"Ot-nay in front of the id-kay," Mary says, with a nod toward Grace.

"I'm not a baby, Mary. I know what a junkie is." Grace's freckled face blazes red. It's easy to forget how young she is sometimes.

Dani drapes her arm over Grace's shoulder, a move that's becoming all too familiar to me. "Yeah, *Mary,*" she says, stretching the name. "She's not a baby. She's one of us now." She flashes me a wink.

I place my pack down inside the ruins and remove the oversized book. "Dani and I have been looking through the spells and figuring out what we want to do next."

Grace tries to keep her distance, but Dani pulls her closer, into the circle. Most of the spells inside require four to cast, and part of me wonders if that's why I invited Grace along in the first place.

Mary runs a finger along the cover. "What kind of spells?"

"Something...bigger," Dani replies. "Something that will change our lives. None of this novice bullshit."

I slide the book from Mary's hand and flip it open, thumbing to one of the pages we bookmarked the night before. "There are spells in this book that can make people do things."

"That's awfully vague," Mary replies. "What kind of things?" It's weird for Mary to hesitate. She's usually the bossy one, but she's more cautious with Grace tagging along.

"It depends, really," I answer.

"The point is," Dani says, "we could use this to our advantage. We all want things, don't we?"

Mary takes a seat by the wall under the crucifix. "It sounds like you've already got a plan."

Grace creeps closer to Dani, never taking her eyes off the book.

I smooth down the page. "Yes, we do, and we'll need to get ingredients for the spell."

"What kind, and where are we gonna get them?" Mary asks.

"We can buy some of them. Some others we need to collect or find."

"Collect?" Grace is practically hiding behind Dani.

"Yeah," I say, pointing to the open page. "We'll need a personal item or something from the person we're casting the spells on."

"Something like this." Dani reaches into her pocket and pulls out the mouthpiece for a vape pen, placing it on the stone I've come to think of as our altar.

"Where'd you get that?" Grace asks.

"Swiped it off Skeet."

"Oh..." Grace nods. "And we can pick anybody?"

I wonder for a moment who Grace might want to hex. I doubt she'll go through with it. Hell, I doubt she'd even have come if it wasn't for Dani. "Sure. Anyone you like. And when we have all the ingredients, we'll come back here and do the casting."

"Shh!" Mary stands, pressing a finger to her lips and looking over the crumbling wall of the church.

I grab the book and stuff it in my bag. Most likely she's heard a squirrel or a chipmunk, but on the off chance someone has come out here, I don't want them to see it.

We all crouch, unmoving, for what feels like an eternity, when voices echo through the forest. I creep to the wall and peer over it. I can make out silhouettes in the distance, heading toward us. Whoever they are, they're carrying something large.

CHAPTER 8

DEEPENING GRAVES

My last glimpse of Elaine as we leave the cabin has her in yellow marigolds, hair tied back with a floral-print scarf. She doesn't look like a woman who's about to scrub blood off a hardwood floor.

We wrap Peej and friends in blue tarp, secure them with bungee cord from Triss's roof rack, and load them into the back of the pickup they drove down in. I contemplate the blood under my fingernails as Triss drives. There are advantages and disadvantages to living outside of town. More chance of a trio of rednecks invading your home, less chance of being spotted when you go to bury them.

"What's the plan?" I ask.

"We're going to church."

"Feeling guilty?"

"Remember that ghost town near the old pits? We bury them in the churchyard there. No one goes to that place anymore. Even if someone did notice the dirt had been disturbed, they'd think it was critters or something. Best place to bury a body is someplace where bodies are already buried."

"What about the truck?"

"Park it by the pits and leave it there."

I nod. She's creating a narrative that the professional in me can appreciate. Peej and his friends go out hunting scrap in the old mine and vanish into the darkness, like so many before them. They won't be missed. Their only connection to the town these days is Mudder's Hole, and I'm pretty sure they don't tip.

"Long hike back home," I mutter.

Triss grunts and doesn't answer. I've already lost her. She's thinking about her wife, alone in the house with no magical barrier to keep her safe from a town caught between a god that doesn't make mistakes and a book that tells them sometimes love is wrong.

The old church isn't one of those modern builds. It's not a piece of a community jigsaw puzzle. The mining town cowered in fear of that place, kept it at an arm's length, until even the walk down the muddy road was an act of penance. The steeple looms, refusing to submit to the encroachment of the forest, refusing to let us forget that we are sinners.

I have a number of reasons to avoid churches, but one always stood out. I never felt loved when I stood inside them. Instead, I felt nothing but a queer constriction of my heart and soul, and I always wondered if what the others were praying to was really what the preacher *said* they were praying to.

Triss swings the truck around and backs through the gate, clipping a crumbling wall and turning it to rubble. The desecration doesn't even flicker in her hard eyes as she brings us up to the edge of the yard. The few intact stones are weathered and illegible; even the mourners have been mourned. There is no one left to feel the weight of all this loss. Peej and his friends will join the forgotten.

Triss flips down the tailgate and tosses me a shovel she took from her garden shed. My lungs hitch at the thought of all that digging. Just for a moment, I wonder if I'll survive this.

"Six feet would be best," she says, taking her own shovel. "Less chance they'll get dug up."

"Right..."

I look at the shovel in my hands, the hard-packed and briar-strewn earth, the neatly packaged corpses in the truck bed. It all seems so incongruous. How am I going to do this?

"Here," Triss says, and starts to break ground by a stone that's still mostly intact. "This guy must have been a rich fuck to afford a slab this fancy."

I join in the excavation. The logic is sound. We don't want to disturb the eternal rest of a kind soul, and every rich man has a thief somewhere in his family.

I'm so focused on the job, on the gauzy crackling in my chest, I don't notice that we're not alone until Triss stops digging. I turn to look but my head's already spinning and the sweat's sticking my blouse to my back. I lean on my shovel to keep from falling.

Twenty years ago, four girls killed a rabbit in the forest because a witch told them they'd have power. They did, for a time. Power and magic, love and success, shame and regret.

Standing behind me, between the half a hole we've dug and the decrepit church doorway, is us. Mousey and meek, awkward and unsure, hungering for something more than what we'd been allotted. I look into that living, breathing mirror and freeze. The thought that we've been caught burying three men—neither living nor breathing—doesn't even occur to me.

One of them's a couple years younger than the others. Elaine was our baby and I wonder if Triss sees the similarities. She looks at me, looks at the shovel, looks at the bundles in the truck.

"Oh my God, what are you *doing*?" the youngster asks.

"Jesus, what does it *look* like they're doing?" another girl replies. There's an affected boredom to her, but I can see the sparkle in her eye. Something interesting is finally happening. How long has she been waiting for a moment just like this?

Did they bring the grunge look back? When was the last time I wore flannel? I don't even realize I've zoned out until Triss nudges me.

"You ain't supposed to be here, girls," she says. "Dangerous out in the woods all alone."

"Is that what happened to them?" a third girl asks, nodding toward our cargo. There's something so familiar about her that I can't place. That hair, those eyes. Who does she remind me of?

I wonder if she'd be so cocky if she could see under the tarp.

"They were bad men," Triss says. Apparently, we have decided not to lie to these girls. I guess it's smart. I'd have been pissed if I was their age and two obvious murderers tried to tell me they weren't burying bodies right in front of me. "They came into my house and tried to hurt the woman I love. This world's better off without people like that."

"Yeah," Grunge Girl mutters. "It's like that with some people."

A moment passes and I can't tell if we've reached an understanding with these kids. Then Triss cocks her head, staring at the third girl, the one I feel like I've seen before, a long, long time ago.

"Hey, I recognize you," Triss says. "I saw you cleaning at the Mason house, right?"

"So what?" the girl asks, but her face starts to burn, like she's been caught.

The story Triss told me on her deck echoes back to me. The Book of Shadows, stolen. White trash girl, the prime suspect. And here she is, old backpack slung over one shoulder, heavy and square.

Four girls. Four directions. Four cardinal elements.

"What's that in your bag?" I ask, before I can stop myself.

"None of your business."

"Really? Because someone stole a book from a friend of mine, and it'd suck if someone lost their job over it."

Grunge Girl folds her arms. "Right? Wouldn't want anyone to call the police, would we?"

I look down at my hands. Shovel, dirt, blood. Are the teenagers in control of this conversation? My luck really has turned.

"You're right," Triss says, and her tone is suddenly more pleasant than I've heard it in days. "Why get them involved when we can just...help each other out?"

"Help each other how?"

"You want to do magic, right?"

"Triss..." I warn, but no one's listening to me.

"That book you've got there's basically useless without the proper sacrifice. I can tell you what to do. Or I can introduce you to someone who can."

They hesitate, trading glances, searching each other's eyes and faces. Who makes the decisions? Are they all equal? Will one of them choose and drag the others with them? All our lives hang in the balance. I wonder what Triss will do if they refuse. I wonder what I'll do.

I don't think I want to die in prison, but...they're just kids.

"The witch?" the familiar girl asks. "In the big house? Is that who can tell us?"

"Triss, this is a bad idea..."

"I'll introduce you. Just as soon as we have these bodies buried."

"We?"

"Consider this your initiation. See, if you're going to be witches—*real* witches—you're going to need to look out for each other. When you're a coven, you're more than friends. More than family. You stand up for each other. Help each other. If one of you does something, it's on you all. You live and you die, together."

I look at the girls and I see them weighing their options, the same way we did when Belladonna gave us that exact bullshit speech. There's no way they won't agree. They think anything's better than where they are right now, living in that trailer park, surrounded by drugs and booze and garbage, cleaning houses they'll never be able to afford to scrape the rent.

Which of those four starts using? Which of them winds up a punching bag for a piece of shit who says he loves her when he's not knocking her teeth out? Which of them wrecks on the highway heading out of town because it's the only way they'll ever escape?

"We'll be able to do magic?"

"All kinds of magic."

"Make people do things?"

"Pretty much anything you can think of. Even if all you want is for them to leave you alone."

Looks pass between the girls and I'm seeing more nods than I want to. I stake my shovel in the dirt and drag myself out of the shallow grave. I must look like such a fucking idiot, scrabbling around in the dirt.

"I can't be a part of this," I grunt, and I'm not sure any of them even hear me.

Maybe what Triss is telling them is true—they can be witches, do magic, if they have the book and make the sacrifice—but she isn't telling them the rest. That pretty soon they'll be meeting up once a week to hex random people in town just for the hell of it. That they'll sow strife and discord just because they can. That, eventually, the magic will run out and everything they've worked for will crumble to dust and blow away between their fingers, their friendship included.

I make it to the church's gate before Triss grabs my arm. I shake her off and lose my balance in the process. I land on my ass in the mud and the taste of iron jumps onto my tongue.

Just in case I'd forgotten.

"Where are you going?"

"You want to take them to Belladonna? So they can wind up like *us*?"

"And what's wrong with that?"

"Look in the back of that truck and ask yourself that question, Triss."

"I don't want to go to prison. Besides, maybe this is what we need. To get the magic started again. We *need* it, Lori. You've seen what happens when Elaine and I aren't protected from this shithole town. And you *definitely* need it."

She digs a hankie out of her pocket and thrusts it at me. I wipe the red off my lips.

"You're still part of our coven," Triss says.

"I can't drag them into this. They're *kids*, Triss."

"So were we. And we did what we had to do. Just the same way I'm doing what I have to do now to keep Elaine safe."

I push myself to my feet and stagger back into the pillar that once formed part of the church gate. My legs, like my lungs, have turned to liquid. "She lied to you."

"What the fuck are you talking about now?"

"You remember how you and Elaine got together?"

"Yeah. She cast a spell from the book, trying to get that guy from school to notice her and it didn't work. She was so cut up about it and I didn't like seeing her hurt and...it turned out she just didn't *actually* like boys."

I'm already shaking my head. "That's what she told you. It was Anais's idea. Triss, that spell we cast wasn't on any boy. We cast it on you. Elaine wanted *you* to love her."

I can't tell if she knows, intuitively, that I'm telling the truth or if she just always suspected, but she doesn't try to contradict me. Her eyes lose focus and I can see her slotting the pieces together. The little incongruities, the bumps and chips and straight-up holes, that magic smooths over so nice.

Marty must have gone through the same thing.

"The magic's run out now. You're not under a spell anymore. Don't you get it? We were never a family. Never a coven. Belladonna used us for something, and if you bring those kids into this, you're no better than she is."

Triss's slap rattles my teeth. I fall down again and lie in the dirt, groaning. She stands over me, clenching fists, like she's trying to decide if I'm going in the hole too.

She jabs an angry finger at me. "Love is a choice."

She marches back toward the truck, the grave, the four girls she intends to drag down with her, and then maybe push a little further. I clamber to my feet and limp back through the forest toward home, the sound of striking shovels at my back.

"Not for any of us, it wasn't."

CHAPTER 9

THE WEAK LINK

As the older women squabble among themselves, Dani watches them with an expression I can't quite name, but still dislike. I want to get out of this exchange alive, but Dani wants more.

Nothing good can come of this.

I lean in and whisper, "We need to get the hell out of here."

Dani snaps her head around as if I've slapped her. "Are you crazy? They can give us power!"

"If they have so much power, why are they out here in the middle of the woods burying bodies? Why don't they just hocus-pocus them away?"

"Magic doesn't work that way, dimwit." She doesn't mean it, but the insult hurts just the same. She must've seen the look on my face because she takes my hand in hers. "I just think we should hear them out. That's all."

Mary and Grace creep over beside us. All our movements are hesitant, in the hopes that whatever they're arguing about is more interesting than us.

Mary sidles in closer. I wonder whose side she'll take. "How do we even know they're for real? They're probably just lying to keep us from calling the cops."

None of us have cell phones—we can't afford them—but these strange, self-proclaimed witches don't know that.

It's Grace who speaks up in their defense. "They knew about Courtney's book."

The temperature in the forest seems to drop ten degrees when she says it. This must be Dani's influence, because the old Grace would've been terrified of these women.

Dani drops my hand and puts her arm around Grace. "See? Grace's right. Of course they're witches."

"Yeah, well it seems awfully convenient that the book won't work without a sacrifice that they just happen to know all about."

And if their story *isn't* all bullshit, how strange to bump into the exact people we need. Is it luck or fate or coincidence that led them to us?

This whole situation is bigger than playing in the forest with a book. If we enter this bargain, we'll be dealing in death. These women are dealing in death. How many years before we're here, burying our secrets in a forgotten churchyard too?

"Things happen for a reason," Dani says. "If we help them out, maybe they'll help us out. They'll at least owe us a favor."

Mary's gaze fixes on Dani and Grace. "Okay."

I've been outvoted. Part of me thinks I shouldn't have shown them the book in the first place, but that won't solve my problems now. My chickens are coming home to roost, as Meemaw would say. I never thought those chickens would be a pair of middle-aged witches burying bodies in the forest though.

I have one more card left to play in this discussion. "They're probably arguing over how to kill us right now."

Dani smirks, and while I usually love the slight jutting of her chin and the way she draws her lip in, all I feel this time is a pit of

dread opening in my stomach. "Nah, they'll just hex us."

Grace giggles and the sound is the first tremor of an earthquake that's going to pull my world down around my ears. This is stupid. This is likely to get us killed, and we're going to do it. Maybe we are ignorant, redneck trailer trash after all.

Maybe Dani has a point and maybe she doesn't, but there's something terribly wrong here, and it's not just the bodies. Besides, how would she know how magic works? None of us know anything yet, and these women are banking on that.

I can't believe they'd give us something for nothing, so the question is, magic in exchange for what? So we don't call the police? It's possible, but they could've just offered us cash. Dirt and blood aside, their clothes look nicer than what people from the trailer park can afford. They're clearly rich bitches.

The echo of palm against face snaps me back to the present, where people are dead and my friends don't seem to care so long as they learn some magic. I watch the scene like it's a car accident I can't tear my eyes from.

"So much for a coven being a family and all that bullshit."

Dani shrugs. After all, it's no sweat off her back. "Families fight, but they're always there for each other. Hell, Court, just look at Teeny and tell me that's not true."

"Yeah, but I hate Teeny."

"But your meemaw always welcomes her back with open arms, doesn't she? And you're still connected to her. You want her to get clean and shit."

The thing is, family or not, I don't *want* to hate her like I hate Teeny.

Dani watches the slapped woman stagger away. "I'll bet she's the weak link. She probably doesn't want to share their power with us."

The woman's steps are uncertain, almost, but not quite like Teeny when she's been at the bottle. She's as thin as a shadow.

From here I can see the deep-set wrinkles and dark crescents lingering below her eyes.

"I'm going to follow her and see if she'll talk."

Mary nods. "We'll stay here and see what we can find out from the other one."

Not one of them offers to come with me, and for the first time, I'm the odd one out. At least I still have the book. They can't do shit without that. I shift the burden on my shoulder and take off on the trail of the fleeing woman.

She moves slowly, and I'm able to catch her before she gets too far. It's far enough, I hope, that the others won't overhear us. If I know Dani, she won't care anyway. She's already written this woman off as weak, useless.

"Hey, wait!"

She seems surprised that someone followed. She bends and places her hands on her knees, panting for breath. "Shouldn't you be with your friends?"

I can barely stop myself from rolling my eyes. "I'm Courtney."

I meet her gaze and a tingling sensation moves up my arm, leaving goosebumps in its wake. She's looking at me. Really looking. Not the awkward kind of glance you get from most people when you first meet them.

"Loretta," she replies.

There is nothing in her tone to let me know whether she's friend or foe, but I saw the shock and pain on her face when the other woman slapped her, and if nothing else, I understand that kind of hurt. It's how I feel every time Teeny relapses.

Despite her exhaustion, her face is set, her jaw locked in an expression of defiance. A spot of dried blood, older than the others, stains her collar.

Dani is wrong about the weak link. This woman isn't it.

I might as well be blunt. "Loretta, are your friends going to hurt my friends?"

She stares at me with an intensity that freaks me out. I've seen that expression on Teeny's face before, when she's been sober too many days in a row.

This woman has seen some shit.

She shakes her head. "I'd like to say not, but...I don't know anymore, Courtney. I just don't know."

CHAPTER 10

BIGGER AND BETTER

By the time I return to the others, they're already helping push the bodies into shallow graves. This whole situation smells worse than Freddie's gym shorts, and I want no part of it.

Dani watches the older woman with an expression that's equal parts wonder and envy. She believes. And maybe it is real, but that doesn't mean it's good.

I almost say I *want* to go home, but that's too childish. "I need to go home."

Dani's attention turns back to me, her brow knit in concern. "What's wrong, Court?"

"I think we should talk about it first," I answer.

"We've already decided," Dani says.

My eyes narrow. They've already agreed without me. "You didn't wait for me?" I know it's Dani pushing this. Mary wouldn't do anything to put Grace in danger, so it isn't her doing, and even though Grace is a coward, she'll agree to anything Dani asks. "Since when do I not get a vote? That's not cool. I think

we should discuss it before we agree. We don't even know these people."

Dani takes my hand. "I thought this was what we wanted. It isn't just for me or Mary or Grace. It's for *all* of us. I'm tired of Heather making you miserable at school, and Teeny breaking your heart at home. I can fix it for you. We can fix it together."

The older witch steps toward us. "Hey there. Courtney, was it? Don't run off so soon. I told your friends that when we clean up here, I'll show you a spell."

She puts an arm over my shoulder. It's a gesture I know well, the same one Dani uses on Grace.

"We're all in this together now." She turns me away from Dani and leads me a few steps into the graveyard. "We're bonded. You help take care of us, and we'll take care of you. We'll teach you things you never knew were possible."

"We? In case you missed it, your friend stormed off."

Mentally, I kick myself. I have no idea what this woman is capable of. Well, maybe *some* idea. We did just catch her digging a grave.

"Listen, Court. I'm going to get real with you." She looks me dead in the eye, expression solemn, and I realize this might be the first time I've ever been taken seriously by an adult. The first time an adult *needed* something from me. "Loretta has problems. She's sick and pushing the people who love her away instead of letting them in. Some people do that. They self-destruct when they can't handle what they're going through because it's easier."

I think of Teeny and nod. What she's saying makes sense, and I don't want to be like that. I don't want to leave my friends when things start to get tough.

"Besides, she's a writer," Triss says, smirking a little. "She's all about the drama, you know? I think it's just how they are."

Some of her smile leeches into me, and she points to the shovel propped against a gravestone.

"Will you hand me that, Court? We want to finish up quick.

My wife's waiting for me at home."

I pass the shovel and notice Dani watching us. She's wearing an expression I've come to associate with annoyance. My heartbeat quickens as I realize she's jealous. She wants to be the one over here talking to this woman.

"Loretta seems to think you might be dangerous."

"I am dangerous," Triss says, "but not to her. Not to you. We're on the same side. In more ways than one, I think. Think about your life. About your friends' lives. Don't you want to get out of this town? Do bigger and better things? We can give you bigger and better."

"How many of you are there?" I ask.

"Four," she says, and tosses the shovel into the truck bed. "There must always be four."

She's starting to sound like a used car salesman. There must be something in it for her. She's not doing this out of charity or goodwill.

With a hand still on the truck, she looks me in the eye. "I know you want this. It's why you stole the book."

"I didn't mean to steal it," I surprise myself by answering. "I felt drawn to it. Like it wanted me to have it."

The corner of her mouth twitches toward a smile. My confession means something to her. "My friends and I can show you how to use it."

Part of me wonders what'll happen after they show us how to use it. Would we be allies? Enemies? Maybe they need more people in their coven. Do witches proselytize? I imagine these women going door to door like Jehovah's Witnesses, and I stifle a grin.

Behind me, Dani is propped against a headstone, sulking. I feel like I'm always chasing her, trying to keep up and have her notice me. Well, she's noticing now. I look away from her and at the woman beside me.

"Tell me what we need to do."

When we finally leave the church, Mary and Grace invite us over to their place. Since going home and facing Teeny is the last thing I want to do, I agree. I'm pretty sure they want an excuse to talk about those women. Everyone has ulterior motives these days.

Grace pops the popcorn while Mary pulls out a collection of DVDs. All horror, because we obviously haven't had enough of that today.

"Courtney, you pick," Mary says, handing me the stack. Since my chat with Triss, they've all been treating me differently. Even Dani.

I sort through the pile. I've seen most of these several times. I choose *Fear*, because between Mark Wahlberg and Reese Witherspoon, that movie has some major eye candy, and the soundtrack kicks ass. Dani nods her approval at my choice.

Mary strows pillows and blankets on the floor in front of the sofa. "So, you were talking to her for a long time out there."

There it is.

I nod.

"What did she say to you?"

I shrug. "Oh, you know...just stuff."

Grace comes in, balancing a gigantic bowl of popcorn and a six-pack of root beer. She settles in on one side of me and nestles in the makeshift pallet.

Mary squeezes in on my other side.

Dani sits opposite Grace. She normally sits beside me, right in the middle, but she's been distracted since we got back, staring off into space and lost in her own thoughts.

Grace passes the popcorn bowl. "Come on, Courtney. Tell us."

I grin, a little ashamed for enjoying the attention. "She's

going to bring us to meet her coven, and they're going to teach us how to use the book."

"Why does she need your permission?" Dani asks, popping the tab of a can of root beer. "We'd already agreed."

She makes it sound like she's ready to leave me out. She's not used to me being the popular one for once. "Because we need four to have a coven, and because I have the book. Without me, there isn't a coven."

Grace's eyes widen. "She said that?"

She hadn't, but Dani's sulking was starting to piss me off. "Yeah. So, we're going to meet them, hear what they have to say, and learn some magic."

"What do you mean 'teach us'?" Mary asks around a mouthful of popcorn. "We've got the book. What more is there?"

I take a handful for myself, too much to fit into my mouth, and Grace giggles as kernels fall down the front of my shirt. "We might be able to do little things with just the book, but these women have been doing this for years. They can teach us how to do more. Bigger and better spells."

Grace scoots closer and passes me a can of root beer. She looks at me with the expression she usually reserves for Dani. We settle in as the movie begins.

CHAPTER 11

GOOD CANDY

"Courtney" bugs me for the next week. Her face lingers because I know I've seen it—or one like it—before. Hell, maybe *I* saw her at Belladonna's and I just forgot. Didn't pay any mind to the little trailer park girl picking up after us.

It keeps coming back to me, even as Doctor Patel presents me with my new, limited menu of treatment options, even as my insurance gets back to me in record time to tell me they won't cover my treatment.

I'm running out of track. End of the line.

I call the bank, but they won't extend a loan to someone they know can't pay it back. My only option is to give up my equity. They want my cottage. The place fits me hand-in-glove, but I tell myself I can do without it. All I need is a roof over my head, any roof, and my laptop. So long as I have that, I can still work.

I try not to cry as I tell them to list it. The advisor I speak to reminds me that, in this market, I can only expect to make about 70% of the value. They're fucking me and I know it. But they have time that I don't. I need money or the well's going to run dry. No pain meds, no anti-inflammatories, no nothing.

There's a difference between dying and suffering.

I go to the grocery store for the first time in years—normally, if I can't drive out to Whole Foods, I get my produce delivered—and fill a basket with the cheapest shit I can find. I'm walking a tightrope and I need to make sure I die before the money runs out.

A couple of my books are sitting in the trash paperback stand halfway down one aisle. Someone bought them from the publisher and put them up here because I was local and I never even knew it. I want to ask if they're good sellers, or if they've been sitting there since they released. I settle for snapping a photo.

The publisher will probably run a memorial when I pass. They'll make a packet off it, and I won't see a penny. I'd have left it all to the others, but now I'm not so sure. My face still stings from where Triss hit me.

I'm spinning the rack for work other than my own to read when I see her in the next aisle. My heart stops for a second, and I think I'm about to have another coughing fit, but it's not the cancer. It's memories, coming thick and fast.

It's not a mistake. It's her.

Christie.

I utter her name without realizing it and she looks up from the six-pack she's caressing. Her stringy, blond hair hangs lank around her face and her eyes are dark with mascara she should have washed off two days ago. She's wearing yoga pants and a "Slippery When Wet" t-shirt that was probably tight before she lost all that weight.

She's a hot mess, but I can't help that little flutter in my chest.

Her chapped lips tilt into a lopsided smile and she leans forward, like she's trying to make sure I'm not a hallucination. "Lori? Holy shit, fancy seeing you here! What's cooking, good looking? Haven't seen you in, like, years and years and years. Damn, you look...thin."

"Yeah, I've lost weight," I say, because I don't want to talk

about it. "You too, huh?"

"Yup. I was recording over in Boston. Had to get in shape. You know how it is."

I nod hesitantly because I can tell she isn't in shape. She's strung out. Her weight has dropped through neglect, not effort. Her nostrils look scorched, and I wonder what the bandages on her forearms are hiding.

"Recording? As in singing?"

"Yeah. Seemed like the real deal too. Son of a bitch took me for a ride, so I washed up back here. I'm staying with my Momma."

"Back in Shady Acres?"

"Feels like I'll need a straight razor to get out of this town sometimes, you know?"

I try not to look at her bandages again. "You always wanted to be a singer. Like Courtney Love, right?"

She laughs. Not a nice laugh. "I wanted a rock star to fall in love with me and tell me I'm beautiful and talented and buy me a house. I wanted to inherit a shit-ton of money. Dreams only come true for some of us."

I gulp, because she could have had all of that and more if she'd stayed with the coven. We could have made it happen. Is it our fault she ended up like this? Did we abandon her when she needed us? How could we have done anything to help her when we needed so much ourselves?

"You still writing?"

"I am. Actually, this is one of mine." I grab the copy of *Withering Hearts* off the stand and hold it out to her.

She grins. "Wow. A celebrity, huh? You gonna sign it for me?"

"Would you like me to?"

A laugh. It almost sounds genuine. "Hey, I have an idea. How about you and me take these back to my trailer and we catch up? For old time's sake?"

I stare at the beer she's brandishing at me, at the feverish look in her eye. I shouldn't do this. She has problems of her own and I'm not going to help anything by—

"I'd like that."

I cuss myself out as we walk to the checkout, arm in arm. I can't refuse the offer. It's the first time someone's actually *wanted* me there in a long time.

"Home, sweet home," Christie says, kicking the trailer door shut behind her.

She slings her bag on a chair and sets the beer reverentially on the table, then starts digging through the drawers for a bottle opener. I look around the room, trying not to notice the places where the walls are secured with duct tape and glue, or where the gaps around the window frame are plugged with newspaper.

My eyes settle on a photograph in a plastic frame, pride of place. Christie's mom—older, but definitely the same woman— and two kids, a boy and girl, smiling right at me.

The girl is Courtney.

I point at the picture. "Are these..."

"My babies."

"Wow. They look...grown up."

Courtney does anyway. She's a high schooler, at least. I try to do the math in my head and the only answer I come up with is that I waited too long to reach out.

"My pride and joy," she mutters, finding her prize and popping the caps from two bottles. "Everything else I ever touched turned to shit, but Courtney's got her head screwed on right."

"Yeah," I say, thinking about our meeting in the graveyard, "she does."

"What's that look for?"

"I didn't even know you'd had a kid."

Christie snorts. "Course you didn't. You never called."

"Who was..."

"What? Who was the daddy? Aww, I can't tell you that, Lori. A lady never kisses and tells. Course, Freddie's daddy was Donnie Hicks, and we both know he ain't no gentleman."

I don't answer. Donnie was one of Peej's friends back in high school. I wonder if they stayed in touch long enough that Donnie might miss him now he's gone.

"He wanted to take me fishing up at Heaven's Lake. Only some old fart chased us off with a shotgun, so we had to find something else to do. Nine months later, my baby boy showed up."

"So Courtney's..."

Her eyes glitter maliciously as she pushes my bottle toward me. "What? Would it make it hurt less if I told you they had the same daddy?"

It's been so long, but she can still see what's bothering me too easily. I'm starting to feel vulnerable. I tip back the beer in the hope I can start to care less about it.

"Did you love Donnie? Or...Courtney's father?"

She laughs and opens herself another bottle. I drain mine because I don't want to be left behind. "You remember that time we went down to the river with the Nelson brothers to smoke pot, and Billy told you he thought you and he should practice kissing, and you had to explain to him what a lesbian was?"

I nod, but my recollection of the event is slightly different. I remember seeing Christie riding in the Nelsons' pickup, flagging them down, tagging along, mostly so I could act as a buffer between her and the hormones of teenage boys.

"You remember what you said? How you explained it to him?"

"I said I'd rather kiss you."

"That still true?"

She leans forward across the table and that lopsided smile forms on lips I've missed for two decades. I'm overwhelmed by memories of Belladonna's kitchen, back when Christie was a witch like me.

"Y'know, Momma's working and the kids are at school. How about we make this a real party?"

Those words linger in me as she slides her bag over and fishes out a pill bottle. She pops a pair of them onto her palm and I recognize them immediately.

"Oxy?"

"Yeah, girl. I got a friend with benefits down at the drug store who can hook me up with all the good candy. Take a couple of these and the rest of the day don't seem so hard, y'know?"

I do know. Ever since my diagnosis came through, pain management has become my primary issue. As a character, I have become woefully one-dimensional. All I care about is making it hurt just a little less.

I reach for the pills. She jerks her hand back, smirking at me. Then she sticks her tongue out. I mirror the movement and she pops them in my mouth—one, two—grazing my lower lip with her finger in the process.

"Cheers," she says, and downs a couple with a swig from her bottle.

I follow suit. Pretty soon, I'll run out of money to afford these pills. I'm afraid of what'll happen if I don't pass quickly enough.

"I tried to get out of this place," Christie mutters, staring at the shapes the sunlight makes through the brown glass of her bottle. "I really did. I tried to take Courtney away with me, but...I fucked it up. Always fucked it up. Now she's stuck here, just like me, and Freddie too. Judge said I can't have 'em anymore, and the worst part of it is, I get it. Who'd want a shitshow like me for a mom?"

I want to tell her she didn't fuck up. I want to tell her she's not a shitshow. Except I don't know anything about her and she's going to smell that bullshit the moment it's out of my mouth.

She's an addict, a train wreck, a starry-eyed dreamer who'll never give up no matter how many times she gets burned, but she's not an idiot.

"Sometimes, I wish I'd killed that rabbit."

"Funny. Sometimes, I wish I hadn't."

She smiles at me, clinks her bottle against mine. "Here's to a pair of fuckups."

The trailer door bangs. I'm aware that's somehow bad news for us, but I'm hazy on the details and too comfortable to move. The oxy must be kicking in.

"Christina, what are you doing? I told you, no alcohol in the house."

Christie snorts as her mom bears down on us. "This ain't a house."

"Correction. It's not *your* house. This is my home, and my grandkids live here. No alcohol."

"Fine, whatever."

Once upon a time, I did everything within my power to stay at Christie's side, but I *always* tried to avoid her mom. I don't think she ever liked me. In hindsight, I'm not sure she was wrong.

She seizes the remaining beers and starts tipping them into the sink. Christie lets out a scandalized cry and tries to grab them back, but her mother has a body built from hard graft and lack of nonsense. Her daughter is too thin, too frail, to take it from her.

"I asked you to fetch cereal. Did you get cereal?"

"Got distracted," Christie grunts, patting herself down in what I'm certain is a cigarette search. "Ran into an old friend."

Her mom fixes me with a cold glare. Recognition creeps into it and doesn't make it any less frosty.

"Loretta Dandridge," she says.

"Hello, Mrs. Fowler. Sorry for distracting Christina. We were just catching up, is all."

"I'll bet."

The weight of her stare makes me feel like she can see the

oxycodone fizzing in my stomach. She knows I've brought Christie back to her home and let her indulge all the vices she's probably trying to force out of her, like the worst kind of asshole.

"I'm going to take a nap," Christie says, giving up on the idea of a smoke. "Great to see you again, Lori."

She leans down as she passes me, smearing a sloppy kiss to my cheek. She brushes her lips over mine and I can't bring myself to hope it's deliberate. Then she's gone, the trailer barely creaking under her bare feet, leaving me alone with her mother.

"I'll leave."

"I think that's for the best."

She walks me to the door, even steps out with me. She dumps the empty bottles in the trash, but I get the feeling she's more concerned with seeing me off the premises.

"She never told me what you all did to her."

"Huh?"

"That night she came back, bawling her eyes out about some rabbit. She was never the same after. Couldn't concentrate. Always looking for distractions. But she never talked about it. I lost my daughter that day, Loretta. Like all the light in her eyes went out. All the love, all the joy. All she ever talked about with any energy was getting out of this town."

"I'm sorry."

"Don't be sorry if you're just going to bring more pain into our lives."

"I won't."

Even as I speak, I realize I'm lying. I need what Christie's offering. Freedom from pain, from loneliness, from guilt. I know where she is, what she has for me. How do I ignore that?

Maybe I can make a deal with the world. Maybe there can be a trade. Because I know something Mrs. Fowler doesn't. Her granddaughter's about to be caught up in all kinds of trouble, and she needs someone to look out for her.

My bill's come due. This could be how I settle it.

CHAPTER 12

ONE COVEN TO ANOTHER

Every Sunday, while the rest of the town were in church, we met at Belladonna's to work our magic. We hadn't met since the day the rabbit feet rotted and the magic left us, but I knew this Sunday was going to be different.

They're all there when I pull up outside the venerable, old witch house. Anais's car is here, as is Triss and Elaine's. There are also four bicycles dropped carelessly on the lawn. There haven't been bicycles on that lawn in twenty years.

I don't have my invitation for this little reunion, but I'm gate crashing anyway. Someone needs to be the voice of reason in this madness. I don't know how it's ended up as me.

I shove the door open like I belong there. My head throbs from the oxycodone comedown. The pain is sharper and brighter than it's ever been. Even wearing sunglasses, the sunlight feels like a flat screwdriver wedging under the lid of my skull. The cool shade of Belladonna's house is still oddly comforting, even now.

I hate it.

The kids are in the parlor, hugging their backpacks, shooting

looks and barbed questions at each other under their breaths. I remember doing that exact same thing when it had been my turn. Awkward, odd, determined that I'd be that way all my life if I couldn't fix it with magic.

I wish I'd known about small print back then.

I stalk through into the kitchen and see a black-robed figure, hood drawn up, standing by the back door. I fold my arms and fix the best glare I can manage into my shriveled-up eyes.

"So, they've got you playing your part in this too?" I ask, not bothering to mask the disgust in my voice. "Gods, Belladonna, you act so fucking aloof, but you're just as twisted as the others, aren't you? Are you really going to drag another four girls into this bullshit?"

I hear her laugh. Then she throws back her hood and blond hair spills out around her shoulders. Anais turns on me with the biggest smile.

"Wow, I must be even better at playing coven mama than I thought," she laughs. "You couldn't even tell it was me."

I balk, backpedal. "I just... The robe..."

"Just admit it, Loretta. I make this look good."

She's certainly put her own spin on Belladonna's classic look. The simple robe is a nice touch, but she's wearing something that belongs in a Renaissance fair underneath, a tightly fastened bodice and swishing skirt. Is she trying to pass herself off as some kind of relic from the colonial era? Would the girls actually respond to that?

Would *we* have responded to that? Probably. Belladonna danced us like marionettes with a blood-red smile and a flash of thigh. Anais's costume's going to blow them away.

"Besides, *someone* needs to play Belladonna, since she's still out of action."

"And she doesn't mind you using her house for this pantomime?"

"I'd guess not. She hasn't told us to leave. She's upstairs, locked in her room. Fuck knows what she's doing up there."

"Don't bother crying to her, Loretta," Triss says, and I realize she's been there the whole time, sitting at the breakfast bar nursing a glass of wine.

Elaine sits next to her, glaring at me. I'm guessing they had a heart to heart about what I told Triss in the graveyard. Good. They needed to get that out in the open a long time ago. If Triss feels like they can move past it, good for her.

I mean, I think she's an idiot, but maybe that's just because I'm sick of being lied to.

"Wouldn't dream of it," I mutter.

Actually, I'd hoped Belladonna would have already stepped in, already told the others that it isn't going to work. She's washed her hands of our little group even more thoroughly than I'd imagined. We're squatting in her house and she's *still* avoiding us.

What does she know? What, exactly, is she afraid will happen?

"We shouldn't keep them waiting long," Anais says. She sounds excited.

But what comes next isn't something to be excited about.

They drain their wine, fortify themselves. I took a pill this morning to keep myself from being sick, so the vomit just churns around in my stomach as I follow them into the parlor. The girls look lost in the woods, wide eyed and jumpy. I keep expecting them to dart under the nearest piece of furniture and refuse to come out.

Courtney catches my eye and then looks away. I wonder what she has to be ashamed of.

"What's she doing here?" her friend in the cut-offs and flannel demands. Dani, was it?

"Family forgives," Triss says, and don't we just seem like the warmest, fuzziest bunch?

"Consider me a conscientious objector," I say.

"What's that mean?" the youngest girl asks.

It means I think you're making a fucking huge mistake. "I'm here to make sure you feel safe. That all of you have a voice. Anyone who isn't comfortable with this can back out. Hell, you can all back out if you want to, at any time. I want you all to know that you have that option."

"We don't have any options," Dani grunts. "We live in a trailer park. You think it's easy when everyone thinks you're trash? We just want a chance to get out. And if magic can do that for us, that's what we all want."

"Oh, magic can do it for you, dear," Anais says, and she's summoned Belladonna's strange, lyrical accent so perfectly I'd think she was her daughter and not just a stray she adopted, like the rest of us. "It can do whatever you want. It's a tool, but more like a paintbrush than a hammer or a knife. You don't have to shape what's been given to you. You can start over. Paint a new, better picture. Love who you want, get what you deserve, and make what you despise about yourself, about everyone else, just disappear."

"It can do all that?" the fourth girl asks. The youngest's older sister, I'm guessing. "That sounds amazing."

"Yeah, too good to be true," I mutter.

"Loretta's right, of course," Anais says, and her candor puts me on the back foot. She smiles at me and all I can do is wait for her to make her play. "Like anything worth having, it requires sacrifice. It requires you to do something you might find questionable, even evil. But this isn't like anything else in life. You won't go through this struggle alone, only to find more struggle on the other side. You'll go through this together, as a family, and everything will get easier. You'll have everything you ever wanted. Everything you'll *ever* want. Trust me, girls, there isn't a more rewarding, more certain, sacrifice in this life."

"What do we have to do?" Courtney asks, staring at her shoes, and I realize why she was avoiding my eyes.

She's into this, same as all the others.

"I'm glad you asked, Courtney," Anais smiles, and reaches into the hutch at the back of the room.

The rabbit is beautiful. Pure, white fur and bright, red eyes and a pink, snuffling nose. I wonder where she got it. It doesn't look like it belongs here, in this place.

She takes it in her arms and it sits there, placid, like it can't tell what's going to happen. Or like it's already resigned.

"Courtney, you don't have to do this," I say, and I hate the edge of desperation that's crept into my voice. "Other girls backed out before."

"Yes, they did, but you're not going to be like them, are you? You're not going to be like your mom."

I scowl. How the fuck did she find out?

Courtney finally looks up. Her jaw drops and Anais's hook sinks right in. "What are you..."

"Oh, didn't Loretta tell you? Your mom used to be a part of our coven, but she backed out at the last moment. She fell at the final hurdle, with everything she ever wanted within her grasp. Do you think it's a surprise she turned to drugs? To alcohol? I don't think she ever forgave herself."

"That's not what happened," I growl.

It wasn't backing out of the ritual that fucked Christie up. It was knowing that *we* went through with it. Knowing that she'd lost the only four people who understood her and cared about her. It was the next twenty years, as we dodged her calls and forgot her birthday and found excuses to avoid seeing her, because we thought we'd outgrown her.

Only we'd all end up in the same place eventually, wouldn't we?

Anais pulls the ritual dagger out of her robe and twirls it in

her fingers. She presents the handle to Courtney. Triss and Elaine roll out a sheet of plastic over Belladonna's good rug.

"You're not going to be like your mom," Anais says, "are you?"

Courtney shakes her head. "No. I'm not."

I can't bring myself to watch what comes next.

CHAPTER 13

BLOODED

But I do watch it. I want what happens to these girls to be witnessed and remembered. I want the suffering and the pain to be noted. I want at least one person in this room to feel sympathy for them.

To become full-fledged witches, they have to take a life. It starts small, but it'll escalate. It did for us. And the stains won't wash out.

They give the quivering rabbit to the youngest. She holds it against her chest and weeps into its fur. Beads of moisture run down its drooping ears. She looks at the others with blurry eyes and I wonder if she's going to crack, to pull out. Her sister looks like she's a heartbeat away from pulling the emergency break and dragging them both off this runaway train.

Before either of them can speak, Dani says, "Hold it tight."

She holds out a hand to Courtney, asking for the knife. The eagerness in her sickens me, because I remember how it felt to want it this badly. I remember what she's thinking.

People kill rabbits all the time. What's the problem? We eat

meat. It's got to come from somewhere. And this is important. I can change things, change myself. We can all be happy. One dead rabbit for four happy lives. No contest.

Courtney won't relent. She steels herself. I wince, my eyes trying to force themselves shut, but I still see the blade sinking in, the red blotting on the white fur.

Except that rabbits don't die quite as easily as they think. As I thought. It's still alive, only now it's hurt. It starts kicking in Grace's arms. She screams and that sends it into full panic. Her sister latches on and they wrestle it between them. Courtney, whose hands are crimson, drops the knife and Dani snatches it up.

She thrusts the knife in, barely missing Grace and Mary, and the carelessness makes me wonder if she really cares for the other girls, or would she sacrifice them for a chance at everything she's ever dreamed of? Either way, it doesn't get the job done. The rabbit wriggles from their blood-slicked arms and tries to hop away. The sisters grab it by each hind leg, pulling it back, crying and whimpering as it screeches stridently, until the whole thing looks as absurd as it does horrifying.

Courtney climbs over them and pins the rabbit under her hand. The struggle goes out of it, almost like her touch gives it peace. A moment later, Dani does the same, but with the knife. She runs it across the poor thing's throat and then sits back, watching it bleed out. The girls fall into one another, sobbing on shoulders and into hands.

I remember this. The blood, the tears. I remember weeping on Belladonna's parlor floor until she banished us upstairs to the bathroom to wash the sins off and change out of the bloody clothing we were wearing.

I remember scrubbing the red off my skin, standing in a Bates Motel shower, watching the color swirling away down the drain between my feet, and wondering how my hands were ever

going to come clean. Over the years, I'd forgotten there was even blood on them. I'd found other things to distract myself.

Gods, it all comes back to me, looking down at Courtney and her friends, holding each other and not even bothering to hold anything back.

They'll think they're stronger when they come out of this. That this is a bond of friendship forged in the brightest, hottest fire. It's a lie. They're accomplices and that's all, clinging to each other because they think only someone guilty of the same sin can absolve them.

The truth is, you spend years just telling yourself you didn't do anything wrong.

"Did you all remember to bring a change of clothes?" Anais asks, sliding to her knees in the mess on the floor. Her voice is a mother's, though she has no kids of her own.

They nod, happy for any reason not to think about what just happened. She puts a hand on each of them, squeezing just enough to be reassuring, then plays Belladonna so well it's like I'm sixteen again.

"Why don't you girls run upstairs and clean up? A shower and a change of clothes, you'll feel like new women. You'll see. We'll take care of the rest. Don't worry."

Elaine offers to show them the way and they file out of the room. Four girls, caught up in something none of them understand. They think the worst is over.

It doesn't get better. We're lying to them about that.

"That was even worse than I remember," I hear myself say.

"I thought they did very well," Anais says.

She and Triss fold the plastic around the bundle and carry it through to the kitchen. I follow, feeling the burn of bile in the back of my throat. I wish I could be sick.

"Do you actually know how to make the charms?"

"I've checked the book. It's quite simple."

"Yeah, well, you'd better hope so. I don't think they'll want to do it again if you fuck it up."

"You're giving them entirely too little credit, Loretta. They're strong girls. Ambitious. Motivated."

"They're desperate. It's not the same thing."

"Oh, you'd be surprised what people will do when they're desperate."

"And the depths they'll sink to. Seriously, you think starting another coven is the way to fix this? Those girls haven't done anything wrong and you're dragging them into this. If this doesn't work, you'll have made them kill an innocent animal for nothing."

Which might still be better than the alternative.

"It *will* work," Anais snaps, and I can see her own desperation starting to flicker in her eyes. "And the magic's going to come back. This will fix everything."

"Better hope so, before you get served."

Anais glowers at me. They deposit their bundle on the kitchen counter. I expect her to get in my face, but it's Triss who rounds on me.

"Why don't you just get the fuck out, Lori? Seriously, what are you contributing exactly? At least Anais is *doing* something. What the hell are you doing?"

Right now, I'm trying to keep four kids from making all the same mistakes we made. Seems like I'm doing a pretty crappy job of it. Probably about as good as the job I'm doing of dying with dignity.

"Like I said. I'm the conscientious objector. At least one person in this fucking house needs to have a conscience."

"Yes, but whose values does the conscience reflect?" None of us can hide our shock when Belladonna sways into the room.

She's wearing an outfit that might be the double of Anais's, save for the fact that it's authentic, handmade, not picked up from the costume shop on her way to bamboozle four impressionable girls.

The warmth in her smile is like she never forgot about us. Like she hasn't been avoiding us for weeks. Like she'll gather us up in her arms and make all the bad things go away.

It's like nothing's changed. I think I'm the only one that isn't relieved to see her.

"Are these the values shared by the women in this house? Or those set out by the church and the town and its small-minded people?"

"You know I'm not religious."

"Perhaps not, but even the most intellectual of women can still be poisoned by the aggressive demand to conform. You've never shared their morality before, Loretta. What has changed?"

"There's blood on my handkerchief. It makes me think."

"About what?"

"Regrets, mostly. Things I would have done differently." *People I would have stood by. Others I should have left.*

"Would you have gone to your grave sooner, all your achievements undone?"

"Maybe. Not like I've got anything to show for it all. At least my hands would be clean."

"She's full of shit," Triss puts in, glowering at me. "She'll be just as grateful as the rest of us when the magic comes back."

"It's not coming back, Triss. Not for us."

"Oh, now, that isn't true."

We all gape at Belladonna when she says that. She moves past Anais, making her step away without even touching her. She stands over the bloody tarp and breathes deep. She's still smiling and the nausea surges in my belly.

I remember we never saw her working with the rabbit, crafting those totems that powered our magic for the next two decades. Have we graduated now? Is that knowledge ours? Or does it just not matter that we're here at all?

"Why the sudden interest?" I growl, knowing the others

want to ask, but are too afraid in case she pops like a soap bubble. "You've been avoiding us. Now you're back. Why?"

"I didn't realize how much you all wanted this," she says, and she holds my eyes like we're making love. "I want to reward your dedication to the Craft. You've done the hard work already. Let me do the rest."

I snort, because I don't want her to know how deeply those words touch me. Lucky I'm anemic, else I'd be lit up like one of her homemade candles.

Anais and Triss glare at me, but I fold my arms, stand my ground. I'm here to stay. Someone has to make sure this doesn't go too far. That's what I'm telling myself. Honestly, I feel like the brakes are off and we're hurtling over a cliff already.

CHAPTER 14

ALWAYS MORE TEARS

It's evening when we grab our bikes and start home. Grace has been silent throughout the whole ordeal. Dani thinks I'm the weak link, just like Loretta, but if any of us falls apart, it will be Grace.

Every time I close my eyes, I see the blood. I can still hear the screams of the rabbit as it died, terrified and full of pain. Who knew rabbits could scream? But they do, and now I'll never unhear it.

"Where to?" Mary asks, breaking our self-imposed silence.

"We've got to get rid of the bloody clothes," Dani says. "If someone sees them, we're going to be in a ton of shit."

"Especially since there's a recently buried body in the old church. If the body is found...or a missing person is reported and we're caught with bloody clothes..." I don't finish the thought.

Maybe that was their plan all along, to craft an elaborate scam so we'd take the fall for their crime. The fact I even consider this reinforces how little trust I have in the older coven. I haven't yet shaken the lingering doubt in my mind, the voice telling me something doesn't quite add up. It's all too perfect.

"You watch too much CSI," Dani says, with a half grin. "We'll go to my place. Mom's working a double, and Skeet will be out drinking at Mudder's Hole until they toss him out on his ass."

We turn our bikes onto the access road for Shady Acres and pedal to Dani's trailer. Her mom's Ford Taurus isn't there, and neither is Skeet's motorcycle. I sigh my relief, and we prop our bikes against the carport.

Dani grabs the key from under the mat and turns the knob.

I hadn't been inside Dani's trailer since Skeet moved in. Meemaw didn't approve, and though she didn't say it, she always found excuses for Dani to come to our place instead. The inside of the trailer is a disaster. Fast food wrappers and overflowing ashtrays line the coffee table and in the corner of the room are little brown lumps of what I suspect are cat turds. I'm not sure they have a cat, and I'm afraid to ask.

I feel like absolute shit. Dani's been living like this for God knows how long, and I didn't notice? What kind of friend does that make me?

She leads us through the kitchen to the compact washer unit in the corner and pushes off the pile of laundry strewn across it. We all join in, filling the tub with our mess of bloody clothes. Dani grabs a bottle of bleach off the floor and uncaps it. "Bleach gets rid of blood. It makes it hard to detect."

I grin. "Now who's been watching too much CSI?"

Her eyes meet mine and her face softens. She giggles and it sounds like wind chimes in the breeze before a storm.

Mary and Grace sit at the kitchen table. I move closer to Dani and lower my voice. "Are we okay?"

She tilts her head. There's a chance she hasn't noticed how short-tempered she's been. How avoidant.

"Of course we're okay, Court. I—"

"Goddamn it!" Skeet's voice booms across the trailer.

Dani's eyes widen like a deer in headlights. "Shit. Go! Run!"

Mary and Grace don't need to be told twice. They bolt for the door. I can't leave Dani, so I stand there. His steps are heavy, shaking the singlewide's frame. He's muttering and cussing. Dani looks at me, then at the door.

"Dani!" Skeet appears in the kitchen. He's wearing a dirty white tank top and a pair of boxers. I can smell the booze radiating off him from across the room. "You know you're not supposed to make all this racket while I'm trying to sleep."

Dani, who I've always thought larger than life, shrinks, curling in on herself to try and take up as little space as possible. Her whole body trembles. "Sorry, Skeet. I thought you were out."

He lurches across the room and grabs her neck, lifting her off the floor. He either doesn't notice me or doesn't care that I'm there to witness. She chokes and writhes, tugging at his hands.

My stomach knots in rage. I thought I hated Teeny. I thought I hated Heather and the other kids at school who tease us for living in the trailer park, but I have never known real hate. Not until this moment. I charge him and slam my foot hard into his testicles.

He yelps and grabs his crotch, letting out a barrage of curses.

Dani hits the dirty linoleum, gasping for air.

"You little bitch." Skeet reaches for me, but Dani grabs his legs and sends him sprawling onto the floor beside her. He lands hard, and she rolls on top of him, balling her hands into fists, and punches him hard in the chest and face.

I grab her shoulder and pull her off him. "Let's get the fuck out of here."

It's the first thing we've been able to agree on without question.

Mary and Grace are waiting for us at the door. We grab our bikes and pedal as fast as we can. We make it to the trailer park's entrance before Grace asks where we're headed.

"To the church," I answer through clenched teeth, and we turn off the road into the forest.

Tears stream down my face, making it hard to see the path, but I don't need to see it. I've ridden this way enough times to know it by heart. All the anger I'd felt toward Dani fades to nothing, evaporating along with my tears.

Of course she'd do anything to get rid of Skeet. Who wouldn't? I glance over my handlebars and see she's crying too. I want to wipe every one of those goddamned tears away, and then I want to kill Skeet. I want to bury him in the churchyard, right beside those bastards the older witches murdered.

We prop our bikes against the gravestones. I walk over to Dani and throw my arms around her. Together, we sink to the ground and sob. After the rabbit, I didn't think I had any tears left to shed. But there are always more tears.

I don't know if Skeet would've killed her or not, but why should she have to take that chance? Suddenly, I don't care if the old witches have ulterior motives or not. My desire to leave Shady Acres is a want, but Dani's is a need.

She wipes her nose on the back of her sleeve and looks over at Mary and Grace, plastering on her trademark smirk. "Did you guys see Court?" Dani sniffles. "She kicked him in the fucking balls!"

Her grin sets off a chain reaction. Mary smiles. Grace giggles. And suddenly, the forest echoes with the sound of our laughter.

CHAPTER 15

ALL IN

"Do you still have the mouthpiece from his vape pen?" I ask Dani.

She nods and produces it from her pocket.

"Good." I drape the old tablecloth over the altar and set candles at the four corners. Earth, air, fire and water, just as Triss instructed me. I open the book, and flip to a bookmarked page.

"What are you going to do?" Grace asks, stepping out from behind Mary.

"We're going to kill that asshole," I answer.

The others remain silent. Maybe they don't believe me. Maybe they think I'm angry and need to vent. All I know is that Skeet will never lay hands on Dani again. Not if I can help it—and I can.

"How?" Mary asks. To my surprise, her voice is tinged with curiosity, not fear.

"Something painful," Dani says. She's looking at the book, not at us, as if not facing us makes it easier to talk about something so difficult. "Maybe we should make him shit himself to death."

Grace giggles.

"I think it's better if we make it look like an accident," I say. I've never actually planned to murder someone before. My eyes flit to Dani's face. Black streaks line her cheeks where tears have made her mascara run.

I rip a piece of paper from my notebook and hand it to her. "Write his full name on this."

She takes the paper and my pen, and does as she's told. For once, she seems content to follow my lead.

I light the candles, murmuring the words to call upon the guardians of the north, south, east and west, opening our circle. We've practiced a few times, but we are beyond practice now. I retrieve the two gifts the older coven gave us after the rabbit ritual from my bag. The first is a small pewter chalice. The second, a black-handled knife the witches called an athame. The objects themselves are beautiful. They look and feel expensive, not like the cheap, plastic-handled bowls and knives we're used to.

They'll help amplify your magic, Triss had told us.

If you want your spells to have power, you have to use quality materials, the other, Elaine, had agreed.

I place the chalice on the cloth in the center of the candles. Dani tosses the mouthpiece inside it. She holds up the piece of paper, a question displayed across the knit of her brow.

I read from the open spell book. "Burn it and dump the ashes in."

She holds her lighter to the paper, and it goes up, blackening the edges.

Skeet deserves to die. He needs to be put somewhere he can never harm another person again, but I wonder what price we'll pay by playing God and making that choice. Will our souls blacken like the sheet of paper that crumbles into ash as Dani drops it into the chalice? It seems an appropriate punishment.

"What's next?" Grace asks. Her voice startles me. For a mo-

ment, I'd forgotten she and Mary were there. Dani's safety is all that matters.

"If any of you have second thoughts, now is the time." The candle flames flicker, casting shadows across the stones. I want this spell to work more than I've ever wanted anything in my life. "After this, there's no backing out."

This isn't like saying Bloody Mary three times in the mirror, or even chanting *light as a feather, stiff as board* while lifting each other off the ground with our fingertips. Either the magic will work, and we'll know for certain we have power, or it won't, and we'll know the other coven played us for fools.

Mary takes Grace's hand and nods. Dani tilts her chin toward me in the affirmative.

I lift the athame, admiring the delicate carvings decorating the obsidian handle—four rabbits on one side, a wolf on the other—before I press the blade's tip into my finger. Blood wells from the cut, and I squeeze it into the chalice.

The color drains from Grace's face as she offers me her hand. The memory of the ritual sticks with her like gum in her hair. The idea of having to do something more, to get bloodier, makes her hesitate.

I shake my head. "No. It can't be taken. It must be freely given." I wipe the knife on my jeans and offer her the handle.

Grace holds the blade against her skin, taking deep breaths. After all we've been through, it's hard to imagine this will be where she draws the line. Her eyes flit from one face to another, looking at each of us in turn.

"He would've killed Dani," I say.

It's surreal to me that a few hours ago, I was the one who wasn't sure about all this, but I'd seen the look on Skeet's face when his hands were around Dani's neck. That bastard was enjoying himself.

She got away this time, but what about the next time, or the time after that? It's a risk I'm unwilling to take.

Mary nods to Grace. "We're a coven now. A family. If someone fucks with one of us, they fuck with all of us."

Grace winces as the knife bites down. Crimson against white. She sways on her feet, and Mary puts an arm around her.

Dani kisses Grace's cheek, then takes the knife. She repeats the gesture, cutting deeper than necessary. I've seen the scars on her arms; she's used to blades against her skin.

Mary takes the knife last. Unshed tears collect in the corner of her eyes. "I'm sorry I ran. I should've stayed with you." Mary's like that. Always trying to be the group's big sister.

Dani shrugs, nonchalant. It's part of the mask she presents to the world. She doesn't want us to know she needs us, but she does.

"Are we all in?" I ask, as Mary puts the athame on the cloth beside the chalice.

"Yes," the others answer.

The sun begins to set, lighting the sky in shades of purple and pink. I inhale the smoke from the candles, committing everything about this moment to memory: The angry red marks on Dani's neck, Grace's nervous shuffling, Mary's confidence.

We join hands and begin to chant.

CHAPTER 16

CHERRY PIE

I used to spend my days in coffee shops in Richmond, my nights in wine bars and restaurants. Then there were the nights I'd sit in my cabin, listening to the wind through the pines and trying to summon memories of my impoverished youth through a lens of gentrified pretension. I'd put it down on paper in the hopes my critics would think it was real enough to praise, but not so real it disturbed them. The rage of Caliban and all that.

Tonight, I'm sitting at the bar in Mudder's Hole, nursing a beer because alcohol is alcohol, peeling off the label by degrees, and smiling at Christie every time she walks into my eyeline. Half the time she doesn't notice, which I guess is karma.

It's probably also karma that I have to watch her flirting with half the dickhead good ol' boys who come in. That I have to endure the cat calls they reserve for the shirt knotted at her breasts and the way they lean forward to get a better look when she bends at the waist to grab a beer from the fridge. I know it's probably part of the job—experience optional, tits essential— but jealousy and wounded feminism are a potent combination. Just add booze.

She pours a whiskey for the latest pig, and he grabs her wrist in a hairy trotter, snorts something into her ear, then pushes a pen and a beer napkin to her. She scribbles what I assume is a nonsense selection of numbers and passes it back with a knowing smile.

Ham on rye takes his drink to the pool table. He pulls a vape out of his pocket, then realizes the mouthpiece is missing and pockets it with an irritated grunt. Looks like he's been in a fight. Fresh bruises are rising around his eye and mouth, but he probably just thinks it makes him look dangerous. Capable. You should have seen the other guy.

Christie walks back to me, like this is her corner and I'm going to towel the sweat off her forehead and cut her black eye. Her smile diminishes by degrees.

"Fucking asshole," she grunts, once she's sure only I can hear her.

"Aren't they all?"

Mudder's Hole caters to a specific kind of clientele. Truckers, bikers, locals and louts—they all wash up here. They drink, they fight, they lech on anything with breasts and they play the same fucking songs on the jukebox over and over again. Christie told me they used to have live music here once, but there was an "incident". Now it's just the jukebox.

Kill me now.

"Skeet's special," Christie sneers. "Everyone knows he's got a steady girl. Mom of one of Courtney's friends. Dani, I think."

I nod. Dani, the punk rock girl. The wannabe leader—Anais of the new generation—except that Courtney's smarter than her, and probably wiser too. Just a shame she seems so committed to making her own mistakes walking down this road.

Not like I can fault her there. In her shoes, I did exactly the same thing.

"Reckon he steps out on her every time he leaves their

fucking trailer," Christie spits, and I get the feeling she's probably laced a couple of glasses with that saliva tonight. "Half the reason he moved in there was because he was looking for a little mother-daughter action. Piece of trash."

As if to illustrate the point, Skeet slams a coin into the jukebox. "Cherry Pie" comes spilling out. I groan. I've heard it already. A couple of times.

"You ever think about telling her?" I ask Christie, since she doesn't seem inclined to walk away. "Dani's mom, I mean."

She shakes her head. "Crazy bitch'd dot my I's and cross my T's. She was never right after her old man passed. Skeet's just the latest. Pretty sure she'd just think I was trying to steal her perfect new guy away."

"Jesus…"

I've written about shitty relationships like that in the past. I guess I always considered myself a commentator. Now I feel like I've just been dining out on the misery of people in my own backyard. I'd like to write Dani's mom a happy ending where she ditches her toxic boyfriend, cleans up her act, reconnects with her daughter, all that Hallmark crap.

Hell, Christie's happy ending has been writing itself in my head since our reunion in the grocery store.

I am drifting in a sea of powerlessness. I am a voyeur in my own life. I can't save them. I can't even save myself.

"You're looking kind of rough," Christie says.

I want to disagree with her, but I saw myself in the mirror that morning. My hair's thinning—I scoop wads out of the sink every time I shower—and pretty soon I won't be able to comb it over the bald patches anymore. The pain has receded to a dull throb, but that's because of pills like the ones Christie presses into my hand.

If her boss catches her dealing, she'll probably get fired. Then again, maybe not. She might be able to work something out. My skin crawls.

"I'm selling the cabin," I tell her.

"Sorry to hear that," she says, and the sympathy is genuine, just not extravagant. After all, she's always lived in a trailer. "I know you always dreamed of a little place like that."

"I've got maybe a week. Then I don't know what the hell I'm going to do."

"It's just you, right? Get yourself a singlewide in the park. You'll have space. A roof is a roof, right? Even if it is aluminum."

"I guess."

"It'd make sleepovers easier," she says, and lays a hand on mine. I want to believe she's genuine, that she doesn't just want a place to drink and get high out from under her mom's watchful eye. Honestly, I'll take what I can get at this point.

"I'll...call about it," I mutter. I can't meet her eye.

Back to the trailer park. I was so terrified I was going to die there, I did terrible things to avoid it. Now it looks like I was always meant to wind up there.

Someone's laughing at me. Maybe the same thing that hovered over the old church and used to eat people's prayers back in the day, long before we buried those bodies in its unhallowed earth. Or maybe something else. Something that's been following me the whole time, and I never opened my eyes to notice.

They're wide open now.

For a crazy moment, I consider telling Christie about Courtney and her friends and their rabbit ritual. It's a point of no return. If I tell her, she'll probably go after Anais and Belladonna with a broken bottle, assuming she doesn't just blame me for not doing more to stop her kid from making my mistakes. Not like I could blame her.

And I can kiss the sleepovers goodbye.

"Something on your mind?"

"Yeah," I grunt. "I hate 'Cherry Pie.'"

Skeet's playing pool all by his lonesome. He keeps making eyes at a girl in chapter leathers and she's batting lashes like he has a chance. Which he might, until her old man shows up. Then he'll be shit out of luck. Guys like Skeet are only handy when they're boxing below their weight. I reckon Dani and her mom know that real well.

"Someone oughta fix him," I grunt.

"They will. He'll piss off the wrong dealer or he'll fuck the wrong guy's wife or daughter one day and they'll find him out in the woods wearing a Colombian necktie."

I scoff. She's right, of course. But just for a moment, I miss the way I used to fix people. I miss the power, the ability to play God. A fairer, more just god than folks around here usually got. A god who gave a shit.

I suck back my beer, trying to drown out the clamor of regrets. As I do, Skeet lines up a trick shot on the 8 ball, dressing to impress. He draws the cue back with a smirk, like it's not the only pocket he's getting into tonight.

The chain holding the light above the table snaps, like the damnedest freak accident. Biker girl screams. Skeet doesn't even look around, he just *moves*. The light smashes down on the pool table in an explosion of sparks, right where he was leaning, cue cocked. His whiskey shatters on the floor, more a tinkle than a death knell.

Christie's boss hurries over, swearing, and blasts the smoking velvet with a fire extinguisher that's still up to code through luck more than diligence. *Everyone* is staring at Skeet.

"Holy shit," he gasps, terrified laughter bubbling from his throat. "Did you see that? Fuck, man, I thought I was—"

None of us get to find out what he thought he was. He steps in the puddle of whiskey and his foot skids out from under him.

The side of his head smashes on the jukebox so hard the fractured skull is audible. He slumps down at the foot of the neon tombstone, neck bent so far his head's resting on his shoulder. His glassy eyes ask the wall what the fuck just happened. Blood trickles out his ear and nose.

The song starts back up.

"She's my cherry pie!"

Biker girl starts screaming. Christie's boss yells at her to call an ambulance and she obeys, but can't take her eyes off him. I reckon they'll need the coroner, more likely.

A bunch of the other patrons start whispering, asking how something like that happens to a guy. They talk about how music's always been cursed in Mudder's Hole and just ask the Freedom Riders.

I have my own theories.

Courtney and Dani must be up late for a school night.

CHAPTER 17

EVERY LITTLE THING SHE DOES IS MAGIC

All through the casting, I kept an eye on Dani. She's fragile, though she'd hate knowing I think that.

Mentally, I kick myself. I can't believe I didn't know how bad it was with Skeet. But what haunts me is that, maybe on some level, I *did* know, and hadn't seen it as *my* problem. I knew Meemaw didn't want me staying there, that Dani was staying over more, and that the sheer number of new bruises she sported in any given week were too many.

If you had asked me months ago, I'd have said I loved her, but I didn't know what love was. Not really. Love isn't butterflies in your stomach when someone looks at you. Love isn't doodling your name and theirs together in the hidden corners of your notebook.

Love is casting a spell to murder the fucking bastard who tried to kill her.

I thought, if it was bad enough, her mom would step in, but I'd forgotten not all moms are caring and attentive. Enter Teeny, Exhibit A.

"When will we know if it worked?" Mary asks, shaking me free from my guilt-ridden thoughts.

"I dunno," I say. "I'm not sure what sort of timeline magic works on. Could be days, could be weeks."

I blow out the candles and start packing our things away. Dani pales at the mention of weeks. She slides a fingertip down the sharp edge of the athame.

"If nothing happens in a few days, we'll go to the older coven and ask them to help us."

I don't want to owe those women any more favors, but Dani is worth it. And based on how we met them, they don't seem opposed to murder.

"You're coming home with me," I tell Dani.

It isn't a question. Tonight, I'm not taking no for an answer. Part of me thinks I should invite Mary and Grace. It was our first real spell, our first act of unity as a coven, but I don't want them there when Teeny stumbles in shitfaced after the late shift at Mudder's Hole, and I don't want to share Dani with them either. Not tonight.

We pedal home in the dark, but it's nothing we haven't done a thousand times before. Meemaw has left the porchlight on for us. I remove the leftovers from the fridge and pile a lump of mashed potatoes on top of a hunk of meatloaf and pop it in the microwave. I don't feel like eating, but Dani still looks pale, and I'm resolved to take care of her. I have Meemaw, but who does she have besides me?

The buzzer sounds, and I slide the plate across the table. Meemaw wanders in from her bedroom in her housecoat and slippers. She doesn't ask where we've been. She pulls out her knitting and sits on the recliner, waiting. It's almost like she knows we need her, like we need some adult, somewhere, to care.

The trailer is silent aside from the rhythmic clacking of Meemaw's knitting needles. The microwave announces my dinner is hot, and I remove the plate. When I turn back to the table, a tear slides down Dani's cheek.

"I'm sorry," I say, though I'm not sure what I'm apologizing for. That I didn't help her sooner? That it happened at all? It sounds stupid. I wish I could think of better words.

She wipes the tear away and nods. She doesn't want to talk about it, and I can't blame her. Dani's never been good at "emotional stuff".

We eat in relative silence. Needles click, forks scrape against plates, and I wonder what kind of god makes a world where people get dealt such a shit hand in life. Dani may be a lot of things, but she's not bad. She's always been the first to come to my defense when Heather tries to start shit, and she never asks for anything in return except my friendship. She doesn't deserve all the bullshit she's had to put up with. But all that assumes there's some cosmic force in the world that cares about motives and intentions.

If the spell does work, I don't know if it will make things better for her, but I'm hard pressed to imagine how they might be worse. It isn't like Skeet helps her mom pay the bills. As it is, her mom's working overtime to keep him swimming in off-brand whiskey.

Dani washes our dishes and stacks them in the dish drainer. When she turns back around, I put my arms around her, and she falls against me, sobbing. Her hand tangles in my hair.

"Oh, Courtney."

The click of knitting needles stops. "What'd he do this time?"

"You don't want to know," I say, squeezing Dani against me, hoping she can absorb my love through osmosis. Take it in and make it a part of her and begin to see herself the way I do.

Meemaw grunts as she crosses the living room and enters the kitchen. She opens the freezer and retrieves a carton of Neapolitan ice cream, then grabs three spoons from the drawer. We always divide it up the same way, vanilla for Meemaw, chocolate for me, and strawberry for Dani. Freddie prefers ice cream sandwiches. His loss.

"You know you're welcome to stay as long as you need," Meemaw says.

Dani spoons a sliver of strawberry into her mouth, and the world feels good for a moment. It feels like a world where we're a family, and men like Skeet can't hurt us as long as we're together.

We've reached the bottom of the carton when the screen door screeches open and Teeny staggers into the living room.

"Christina? I wasn't expecting you home for hours. I thought you were closing tonight..." Meemaw stops speaking when she sees Teeny's face.

"He's dead."

"Who?" Meemaw asks.

"Skeet. He was at the bar, drinking and playing pool, and he—" She's clearly in shock. "I saw it all."

Dani and I look at each other, and there's a spark of hope in her eyes. A spark I thought I might never see again.

We have magic.

CHAPTER 18

DANCING WITH THE WIND

The next day, we gather at the church. We're drawn here like a ritual, though I don't know exactly why. Maybe it's the energy, like Dani said, or maybe we just don't know where else to go. Church is supposed to be a place of comfort and hope. After that last spell and what happened to Skeet, I am hopeful.

Maybe we finally get a choice. That's what we're here to find out.

Mary and Grace prop their bikes against the crumbling wall.

"We did it," Dani says. "Skeet fell and bashed his fucking skull in, and we did it."

Grace's eyes are wide like she can't believe it.

"You're shitting me," Mary says, unable to contain her excitement. "Really?"

"Teeny saw the whole thing," Dani continues. "Swear to God."

"Holy shit." Mary laughs in disbelief. "I mean, I'm sorry."

"Don't be," Dani replies. "We knew it would happen. It's what we wanted."

I understand the conflicted feelings. I spent half of last night awake, trying to figure it all out. How it happened, how I felt about it. There's a small chance it could have been a coincidence, but I'm not sure I could sell that story to the others today.

I spread the cloth over the altar and arrange the candles, just like before.

"Think it will work again?" Grace asks.

"I don't see why not," Dani replies. "Clearly the rabbit ritual unlocked our powers. We can do anything now."

"We're going to test it out," I say.

They all turn and look at me as I flick a flame to life on the red plastic Bic I swiped from Teeny.

"How?" Grace asks.

"We all have something we want," I answer. "Dani wanted Skeet dead, and now he's dead. We need to see if this is really real, or if it's some kind of coincidence. We're going to call the corners, and we're all going to ask for something this time."

Mary nods, and Grace looks at her feet. "What sort of thing should we ask for?" she asks.

"Whatever you want. We don't know if this power has limits, so we're going to test them." Part of me thinks we should wait for the older coven, to tell them what we've done and ask them if it's possible, but I've been waiting to be special my whole life.

Dani looks at me like I'm a hero. Like I'm the reason all of this has happened. I've never seen that expression on her face before, and I'm not ready for it to fade.

We join hands and open our circle, just like last time. We pass the athame around, each giving a drop to the chalice. It's easier this time. None of us hesitate. We know what's at stake.

Grace burns and tosses in the ashes of a pop quiz. "I want to make better grades, to get a scholarship, and go to college." She looks at me and hesitates. "Is that too many things?"

I shrug. "No idea."

Mary burns and tosses in a dollar bill. "I want money again. I miss having nice things."

They turn and look at me. I've been thinking all night about what I'd ask for. I couldn't decide, so I take a sheet of paper from my pocket, and show them the side with Teeny's name on it. I burn it and add the ashes to the pile. "I want to be happy."

I don't say "I want her to get clean", for the same reason I don't show them the opposite side of the paper—the one with Dani's name encircled by a heart. I'm pretty sure that in the history of wishes and spells and curses that there's a taboo against forcing people to love you, but murder is probably taboo too, and the magic didn't seem to care.

Besides, I didn't wish for either of them to love me. Not out loud. And spells can't read minds, can they?

It occurs to me that I don't know how magic works, if it's like a computer program that does what you tell it exactly, and only what you tell it, or if there is some subtle art to it, a kind of interpretation of intent. Either way, the spell will fulfill my wish however it sees fit.

Or perhaps my spell is too vague. Faced with uncertainty, maybe the magic will fizzle out.

When we've finished chanting and closed the corners, I blow out the candles and wrap the book in the altar cloth.

Dani waltzes over and drapes an arm over Grace's shoulder. "Do you think it will be fast like last time?" she asks.

No one answers, and it takes me a second to realize Dani's asking me. "I'm not sure. We could talk to the elders about it. Ask them about the rules. I'm not sure if there is a limit to how much power we can draw on, or how many times."

She pulls Grace over and links hands with me, the other hand in Grace's. "Mary, come here." Mary trots over, and we close the circle, hand in hand. "Let's see if we can make anything happen without the book or the altar. Just us, and the rabbit's feet. How about it, Court?"

She asked me, which means she's come around to the idea of me leading our coven. Or maybe she's just feeling complacent after Skeet. "Okay."

"Close your eyes," she says. "Think about the wind. Think about the leaves rustling and your hair being tussled. Think about pine needles blowing around your feet."

My neck tickles, and I move to brush it, but Dani squeezes my hand tighter. "Concentrate. Now say, 'We summon thee, spirit of the wind.'"

"We summon thee, spirit of the wind."

A light breeze brushes my skin.

"Again."

"We summon thee, spirit of the wind."

A gust blows so hard it almost knocks me off balance. Dani laughs, and we open our eyes to see a cyclone of wind and leaves blowing up between us.

"Holy shit!" Grace shrieks.

"Holy shit," Mary echoes, in a lower voice.

We follow her gaze. The wind has kicked up enough leaves to uncover a small trap door in the floor of the church. It's half rotten, and it's only by pure luck that none of us has stepped on it before.

We drop hands and the breeze dies down. Mary falls to her knees and tugs at the ancient door. It practically disintegrates in her hand. Under the door is a small chamber, not large enough for a person to fit inside.

Mary sticks her hand into the hole and fumbles around in the darkness. After a few seconds, a wide grin stretches across her face, and she pulls out an ammo can.

"What's that?" Grace asks.

Mary pops open the latch, and we give a collective gasp. The box is stuffed with rolls of money. Literal wads of cash, and plastic zip bags containing a white, powdery substance.

"It's someone's stash," I say.

"How long do you think it's been here, right under our feet?" Grace asks.

"Years," Dani says. "You saw how that door fell apart when she touched it."

Mary unrolls the cash, counting the money. "The spell worked. It worked already. Just like that!" She laughs. The whole scene looks like something out of a cartoon.

"Don't forget the drugs," Dani says. "I'll bet Teeny could get us a fortune for them."

The mention of Teeny's name is an icicle stabbing my heart. "Absolutely not."

Dani walks over and takes my hand in hers. "Court, it's a sign. You've done this. You've made it happen."

I want to cry, but I also want to melt into her smile.

CHAPTER 19

What Manner of Bliss?

Skeet's funeral is sad. Not sad in the "grieving friends and family" way, like most funerals, but sad because less than ten people show up to see him off to the afterlife. The church is small, and not one I recall him having ever attended. I'm not quite sure how that works, but regardless, the priest delivers a few generic words about God's mercy and forgiveness.

Skeet's gonna need all the forgiveness he can get.

I came because Dani asked me to. She's wearing a flannel shirt unbuttoned over a black dress, and her mascara is caked so thick her eyelashes are like spiderwebs. It makes me think of the black streaks of her tears, but there won't be any tears today. Not for Skeet.

Dani's mom, Marlene, uses her grieving as an excuse to rewrite history. Skeet was a good man, a good provider and—get this—a good father to Dani.

Fuck that revisionist history bullshit. But I guess if making Skeet a good man retroactively helps her, what harm can it do? We all pretend. Like the way I pretend when Dani reaches for

my hand that it means something more than "thanks for coming with me".

I can't do it alone, she'd said, when she asked. *You know I'm no good at emotional shit*, and *I can't be around Mom either. She's so empty, and all she wants to talk about is Skeet and all I want to do is sing the Hallelujah chorus now that he's dead.*

Seeing Dani released from her anxiety gives me hope that we've done the right thing. I mean, I know murder is wrong, but is it always? When douchebags like Skeet get to walk around unchecked, what does that say about society?

Dani tugs my hand, signaling it's time to go. I cast a glance at the casket but feel nothing. No, that's a lie; I feel relief.

"Why don't you come home with us, Courtney?" Marlene asks. "Dani and I could use the company."

Dani smiles. It isn't awkward or apologetic like it used to be when her mother invited me over.

"Yeah, I'd like that," I say.

The screen door bumps into my butt as I follow Dani into their rusted-out singlewide. Their trailer is old, even by Shady Acres standards. I take a second before lifting my head, preparing myself mentally. I remember the garbage everywhere, and the smell. But I smell nothing this time, so I open my eyes. The room is clean. No empty bottles or full ashtrays or mysterious brown clumps.

"Whoa."

Dani grabs my hand and pulls me toward the hallway. "Wait till you see my room."

"You got your room back?" I ask in a whisper.

When Skeet moved in, he'd taken over Dani's bedroom as his "Man Cave". When Dani had bothered sleeping at home, she'd been sleeping on the couch.

She leads me down the hall, which has a fresh coat of yellow paint. It's sunny and happy, two things I'd never really associated with this place.

She closes the bedroom door behind us and cranks the window open. The walls are newly coated in slate-gray paint, and the fumes still linger in the air. Skeet's posters of scantily clad women sprawled across sports cars are gone, along with his stacks of magazines and the deadbolt he kept on the door.

"When did you do all this?" I ask.

"When Mom got the call about Skeet, she came home and started cleaning." Dani sits on the edge of her wicker bed, the one they'd moved to a storage unit when Skeet claimed the room. There is a new comforter on top with a skull and crossbones motif. "I got back from your house and found her cleaning and sobbing. It was the weirdest shit I've ever seen. She didn't say anything to me, so I just grabbed a pair of gloves and a garbage bag and started helping. We didn't even talk, we just stayed up cleaning until it was done. The next day she took me to Walmart, and we got all the paint and shit."

"Damn."

She pulls a pack of cigarettes from her shirt pocket and offers me one. I shake my head, and she shrugs, tucking the pack back in without taking one for herself.

"So, do you want to stay over?" she asks, a nervous tremor in her voice. "The paint's probably dry enough to hang stuff up."

She gestures to a pile of rolled up posters in the corner. Mostly bands, though there is an old *Twilight* poster she used to keep rolled up in the back of her closet.

I pick up the first and unroll it. It's the album cover from My Chemical Romance's *The Black Parade*. Vintage, but respectable. The skeletal drum major leading the march sort of matches her comforter.

She grabs the pack of thumb tacks from the top of her dress-

er and joins me, smoothing the poster against the wall. "Did you talk to Teeny?"

She asks me every day. I'd hoped she'd taken the hint before when I didn't answer, but Dani isn't really the subtle type. Eventually, I just went along with it, no matter how I felt about it. After all, the magic had given us that money.

"Yeah, but...it just felt so weird. She's my mom, and those are drugs."

Dani stands on her tiptoes and stabs a tack into the corner of the poster. "Right, but that's all the more reason she should do it. She wouldn't want you going to someone else. And she knows you know she deals. It's this whole giant elephant in the room. Might as well get it all out in the open."

She tacks the opposite side and turns. She's squished between me and the wall. She smells of menthol cigarettes and rosemary shampoo. Her eyes are like puddles of melted chocolate.

"You know, Court, I never thanked you enough for what you did. Skeet's gone. I have all this"—She nods to the room— "and it's because of you. I know it wasn't easy for you with the rabbit. You've always been the sensitive one." She brushes my cheek and tucks a stray strand of hair behind my ear.

I imagine her leaning forward and closing her eyes, but she presses her lips roughly against mine and suddenly, it's not just me imagining it. Her teeth pull and tug at my bottom lip, and I'm so happy I can't even wonder if it's real or a dream I'm going to wake up from.

My tongue draws a line across her bottom lip, and she pulls me against her like she needs this as much as I do.

"I know what I want, Court." Her dress falls into a pool around her ankles. She tastes like cherry Chapstick and cigarettes. "I'm not scared anymore."

It's me.

She wants me.

CHAPTER 20

MAINLINE

I wasn't invited to Skeet's funeral, but I was there. I wanted to keep an eye on Courtney and Dani, keeping to the back, out of view, wearing sunglasses and a baseball cap that did a passable job of hiding my patchy, freshly shaved head. Anyone who saw me probably wouldn't ask too many questions, and even if they *could* identify me, having a reputation for being morbid helps. Folks just think I'm hovering, hoping for inspiration for a new book, sucking up grief from the graveside like a vampire.

Maybe they're right. God knows the others and I have been feeding on this town for years, taking from it and never giving back. We made our offerings so we could be rich and loved and protected from everything we feared. We rose above. Then we kicked the ladder down behind us.

I can't help thinking, watching Courtney and Dani at the grave, that we could have done something for them, to stop it from turning out like this. Maybe if we'd used the magic to make the town better, instead of just making ourselves better off, none of us would be in this mess.

They've got the magic now. In a way, it's karma.

It's afterwards, on the walk back to the trailer park, that I realize more people showed for Skeet's funeral—a piece of human garbage, as Christie put it—than will show for mine. That thought haunts me right up to my door.

It's unlocked when I get home, and I feel a shiver run across my soul. My thoughts are muddled and I'm not careful like I used to be. Sometimes I cross the road and realize after that I didn't look both ways. And sometimes I forget to lock the door.

This isn't one of those times though, because Christie's here, sprawled on the tattered, collapsing leather couch, her spare key on the coffee table next to...

At first, I can't figure out what the plastic baggies on the table are for. Making them make sense is like trying to snatch snowflakes out of the air, and I'm not as nimble as I used to be. Then I remember.

This is Christie. Those are probably drugs.

"You're back! Feels like I've been waiting forever. Didn't want to start the party without you."

"Where the heck did you get all those?" I ask, dumping my purse and kicking off my Italian leather flats. At least I still have decent clothes for a funeral.

Christie's expression creases in vicious delight. "Courtney. Her little friends found them in some old church, under the floor or something. Must have been some kind of stash that no one came back for." She picks up one of the bags and dangles it, watching the white grains inside trickling into its corners. "Like mother, like daughter, huh?"

"Y'know, most moms wouldn't be proud of that."

She scowls at me, and I try to smile like it's a big joke. Christie isn't like most moms.

"Had to bring it here to keep it away from my mom. She'd

have flushed it down the john for sure. And she would've given me hell for it. Might have been worth it to see the look on her face when I told her Courtney brought it home from some place in the ass end of nowhere."

"You wouldn't do that," I say, cold sweat prickling my back. Even to my own ears, it sounds more like I'm trying to convince myself than stating a fact.

"Course I wouldn't," Christie says, with complete certainty. I can't tell if she's lying to herself or to me. I think she stopped caring who she hurt a long time ago, maybe when the pain of being alive became too great.

"Why did she give it to you?"

"Because she knows I've got the hook up. I can sell this shit and we can make a mint off it. We'll be sitting pretty. Won't be enough to get your cottage back, but maybe we can upgrade to a doublewide with windows that actually close. Sounds like paradise, don't it?"

I nod my agreement. It's not the way I imagined mounting my comeback, but my relationship with money resembles my relationship with her. Complicated and needy.

"Could get a car. Put a deposit down on a place. Jewelry and furs, maybe?"

"What about putting some money aside for Courtney's college fund?"

Christie jeered. Always her least attractive expression. "I never went to college, and I turned out just fine."

She examines the baggie in her hand again, thinking thoughts that are going to get us into trouble. I didn't go to college either, and Courtney might not go for the exact same reasons. Because magic's going to make all her dreams come true.

How well did that turn out?

"I feel like maybe we should do a little...quality control, if you know what I mean. Can't sell it if we don't know how it is. That's just good business."

"I thought good business was, 'Don't get high on your own supply'. Besides, since when do you take anything that hard?"

Christie just laughs at me. "I keep forgetting, you weren't around during the glory days. Girl, this is the after party. I've done all kinds of shit. C'mon, let me cook you something up."

"Let me hit the shower first. I need to get the funeral stink off me."

"Want me to come wash your back?"

She grins at me over a coffee mug full of Jack and Coke—the Coke bottle's barely empty, but the whiskey's nearly gone—and I don't admonish her for flirting. The way she torments me just feels like part of my penance.

I think it's why I gave her the spare key, why I let her crash here whenever she wants. She gives me a taste of something I always wanted but gave up for something I thought I wanted more. Now I know I can never have it, and these moments help to remind me that I'm in a hell of my own making.

And it's nice to have company.

I shed my funeral suit carefully, aware I can't afford to waste money on getting it laundered. I need it to look good in case they bury me in it. It's a lizard skin I habitually molt, but I keep it around because grief makes it fit, here and there. It's pretty loose now though, since I started grieving myself.

Standing under the water—even the terrible pressure in the trailer park makes me feel like every drop is going to leave a bruise—I try to piece together the snowflakes I caught from Christie. Courtney and her friends found drugs. They gave them to Christie to sell. I guess it's nice they're reconnecting. They were never going to be like normal families.

I think about her heating the spoon, prepping the syringe,

digging surgical tubing out of her bag. Do I want this?

The answer to that question isn't as compelling as the fact that I *don't* want the rest. Whatever works, really.

I remember seeing baggies just like those—exactly like those, with the same colored stickers—in Brad's glovebox. They fell out and scattered on the ceiling of his car after he flipped off the road. We left him in the driver's seat, drowning in his own blood, while Triss freed Elaine from the trunk and carried her home.

Felt good watching him die. Righteous. He was a piece of garbage—like Skeet, come to think of it—and Elaine hadn't been his first victim. At least she'd walked away from it.

What was the other girl's name? Lynne? Linda?

The fog lifts, just for a moment. Lynette, one of his regular customers, wide eyed and blue in her bedroom with a needle in her forearm.

Little bags of death. That's what I'd thought, looking at them scattered around his car.

Two snowflakes melt into one in my palm. I snatch a towel off the rack and I'm still binding it under my arms as I sprint out of the shower cubicle.

I'm too late. Christie's sprawled on the couch, head back, eyes wide, rubber tubing curled in her fingers and the needle point-down in the carpet like a dart. There's white froth in the corner of her mouth. I grab my purse, start raking for a phone I sold to buy bread last week.

"Fuck!" I scream, and hurl my bag full of useless shit across the trailer.

There's only one other place I can think to go. I leap out, still wearing only the towel, and almost slide over in the mud outside. I think I step on a shard of broken bottle, but terror and opiates numb everything but the brilliant spike of adrenaline.

The park passes in a blur, and then I'm bruising my hand

against the door of Christie's mom's trailer, yelling for her at the top of my lungs.

Where is she? Doesn't she know her daughter's dying?

She throws the door open before my impatience can give way to full-blown panic. She's ready to cut me, but the razor of her tongue falls still. She must see the fear in my eyes. I don't have time to thank her for the reprieve.

"Call an ambulance. Right now!"

CHAPTER 21

Fool in the Rain

The word "overdose" hits me like a ton of bricks. I should be sad, but I'm mostly numb. What do Janis Joplin, Layne Staley, Scott Weiland, and my mom all have in common? None of them ever loved me, that's what.

I'm a spoiled brat for feeling this way, for making it about *me*. I know it isn't about me, because nothing Teeny's ever done has been about me.

But I gave her the drugs. I let myself get caught up in Dani's fantasies of money and escape, and the kisses all those promises were lined with. As it turns out, hope is a drug too.

Meemaw sits beside me on the sofa, holding my hand. "Do you want to ride down to the hospital and see her?"

"No."

It's not my fault, but it is my fault. I knew who she was when I passed her the baggies. I saw the eagerness in her eyes. Meemaw had shown up at Dani's trailer to pick me up and tell me Teeny was in the hospital.

Dani hasn't spoken to me since. She hasn't called to check on

me, nothing. It hurts, and I'd take it more personally if she wasn't constantly reminding me of how bad she is at "emotional stuff". Maybe she thinks she's giving me space.

Maybe, after Skeet, she's giving herself space.

I trace a finger along the faded floral patterns of the cushions.

"You sure?" Meemaw asks, squeezing my knee.

"Why is she like this?" My voice cracks and my cheeks are suddenly wet.

Meemaw pulls my face into her chest and hugs so tight I worry about being able to inhale. "She's just sad, baby. Seems like she's been sad for most of her life. Sometimes the drugs help her forget how sad she is."

I sniffle, and I know I sound like a baby when I ask, "Why doesn't she try harder to be happy? For us?"

Sobs rack Meemaw's chest. I don't know how long we sit like this, crying and empty, before the phone rings. Meemaw picks up the landline.

Someone mutters something official-sounding and she says, "This is she." More muttering. I hear Teeny's name. "Uh huh." A pause, like they hesitate, and then a statement.

Something that makes Meemaw sigh. "No insurance." Confirmation. Then they ask her a question. She sighs again, heavier this time. "Yes, you can send the bill here. Look, is she stable?"

They answer straight away, and I see her eyes narrow with anger.

"What do you mean that isn't your department? You have the nerve to call here asking about money, and you can't even tell me if my daughter is *alive*?" I'm not sure if the person on the other side has a chance to reply before Meemaw slams the phone down. "Bunch of goddamned vultures is what they are."

"Remind me never to piss you off," I say, wiping tears away with the back of my hand.

Meemaw guffaws, and for the first time in days, we laugh.

"You know God never gives us more than we can handle, right?"

I can't bring myself to tell her I haven't believed in God since I was twelve, so I nod instead.

"I think I'd like to go out. I promised Grace I'd tutor her, and I've been doing a crap job of it. I think it'll help me take my mind off stuff. Would that be okay?"

After our spell, Grace's grades have been on an upward trajectory, so she maybe doesn't need me, but it's something to do.

Meemaw nods. "Ain't nothin' we can do for Christie just sitting here. I might go up to the hospital later and stay with her. Freddie is staying overnight with one of his little school friends."

"Did you tell him what happened?"

She shakes her head. "And don't you do it, neither. He'll learn what she is sooner or later, if she don't kill herself before then. No need to rush him. For now, I told him she's away with a friend."

"Loretta?" I ask. I wasn't going to broach this subject with Meemaw, but it might be now or never.

"Yes." Her answer has an edge. "You've met her?"

I study a brownish stain on the carpet. Probably spilled coffee. "Yeah."

"Courtney, I want you to stay as far away from that woman as possible, do you hear me?"

I trace the edge of the stain with my thrift-store sneaker. "She seems nice."

Meemaw adjusts herself to face me. "She may seem like a lot of things, but let me tell you something... A long time ago, when Christie was your age, she wasn't the way she is now. She had a group of little friends, and that she-devil was one of them. I don't know what they did to her, but whatever they did...they stopped speaking, and that's around the time Christie picked up drugs for the first time. She never did tell me what they'd done to her, but you see what she's like? I lay that sin directly at the feet of that woman and her friends."

"Maybe she's changed?" I offer.

Meemaw snorts. "You're smarter than that, Courtney. You think it's a coincidence that woman shows back up and now Teeny's in the hospital with an overdose? It ain't. That woman ain't never been good for Teeny, ain't never treated her right. Broke her heart."

Breath caught in my throat. It's the closest Meemaw has ever come to acknowledging Teeny's sexuality. When people mention it, whether in whispers or to her face, Meemaw always retorts with, "Ain't none of your business what people do behind closed doors unless they invited you."

It's always been an open secret.

I wonder if she knows how I feel about Dani. I wonder if people whisper about us, and if Meemaw tells them to mind their own damn business too. My chest tightens.

Meemaw's still speaking. "...just dumped her. Never came back to check on her, even in bad times. What kind of friend does that? Just abandons someone when they need them the most?"

I take Meemaw's cold hand in mine and give it a squeeze. "I'll stay away from her. I promise."

She kisses my forehead. "You go on out and have fun with your friends. Don't you worry about Teeny; her decisions are hers alone. They ain't got nothin' to do with you or me."

CHAPTER 22

BLUE ON BLACK

I've spoken to too many cops recently. After Skeet's death at the bar, and now, at the hospital, with Christie fighting for her life in the next room. No way they were going to overlook that much heroin on the coffee table. Intent to distribute, that was what they'd called it.

And what did I do, knowing she couldn't contradict me? I threw her under the bus. Abandoned her.

Again.

I told them I didn't know about the drugs. True. Told them Christie had brought them into my trailer but that I hadn't seen them before I'd jumped in the shower. Lie. Told them I didn't know where she'd gotten them. Lie, but maybe she'd forgive me for that one.

They'd tie them back to Brad eventually, assuming they weren't complete morons. It'd mean they wouldn't think she was a chemist, but they wouldn't ignore the fact she hadn't just gone straight to the police. When she woke up, she was looking at doing time. Could she survive that? Could I?

With Christie in my life, I could wallow and forget about what's been happening with my old coven. Now I don't have that option, and I need to do something about all these regrets piling up.

Getting to Anais's fortress on the hillside is tough without a car. Tougher without my health. I walk until my feet are numb and my calves are burning and my lungs are rattling with every inhalation. I hack and spit red whenever I stop to drag oxygen into the muslin bags my lungs have become. I leave pieces of myself all over the forest and I worry about what might find them.

More and more, I'm getting the feeling of being watched, of footsteps matching mine, stopping when I stop to listen. Maybe I'm hallucinating—some of the stuff Christie gave me, the stuff I managed to hide from the cops who searched my trailer, is pretty strong—or maybe I'm externalizing my antagonist, so I can fear something other than my body.

Or something really is following me. Witchcraft is real. Why not monsters? Why not the Devil?

Marty's car isn't in the drive, but Anais's is. Good. If I'd wasted the journey, I'm not sure I'd have the energy to get back to the trailer park. I prop myself against the mailbox and wonder, for a moment, if I'm going to die here. If I pass out, no one'll find me until it's too late.

Then I breathe deep and something pops in my lungs that terrifies me but also makes it easier. I am borne up by a sudden burst of clarity and I make my assault on the dragon's lair.

I'd love to kick the door in and demand answers, but in the battle between the strung-out cancer patient and the solid oak security door, I think I know which side wins out. So, I ring the doorbell and savor my defeat.

When she doesn't answer, I knock and holler, "Anais!" I'm pretty sure I go blue in the face as well.

It's a full five minutes before she answers the door, and when she does it's slow, guarded. Alarm bells start ringing, even before I see the purple storm cloud around her left eye.

"Jesus, Annie. What the fuck happened?"

She takes a shaky breath and pulls the door open so I can step inside. The moment I'm on the doormat, she throws her arms around my neck and buries her head in my scarf. She'd probably get all tangled up in my hair if I hadn't shaved it off a few days back. I was getting sick of seeing how ragged I looked in the mirror. At least this way I look like Sinead O'Connor, just without the good faith.

"I d-don't know what happened, Lori. One minute we were j-just talking and then h-he...he..."

She breaks down in my arms and I don't have the heart to tell her she's hurting me, that I'm going to fall if she doesn't take her own weight soon. I feel apologies bubbling in my throat like the blood I've been spitting these last weeks. I should have listened to her, about Marty, about all of it. I should have...

Something changes in the way her body shakes that gives me pause. The sobbing takes on a new cadence, and I've heard my sisters in tears enough times to know that this ain't them.

It almost sounds like she's...

"Why the fuck are you laughing?"

I pull away and Anais throws her head back, cackling, crocodile tears drying on her cheeks. It's not the first time in recent memory she's made me feel like an idiot for thinking she was being sincere. My cheeks sting where the blood's rushed in, and I'm surprised I have enough to be embarrassed.

"What do you think? Oscar? Academy Award?"

"What is even wrong with you?"

"Nothing's wrong with me, Lori. Pretty soon, everything's going to be just perfect. We're going to fix this mess." She kicks the door shut and waves me into the kitchen. "You want a drink?"

I follow her dumbly to the breakfast bar, where wine bottles form ranks beside glasses stained with her lipstick and tears. Has she been practicing? She starts shaking bottles, looking for one that isn't empty.

Thoughts don't come so easily anymore. It used to be like checking things off in my journal, reading back through the pages when I needed something. Now it's like someone shredded it all and I'm trying to piece it back together. But I only need a few pieces of this to start to form a picture.

She wanted to death hex Marty, wanted him gone before he could file for divorce. With him dead, everything comes to her—the house, the cars, the money, probably a sizable life insurance policy. Marty was careful enough to make her sign a prenup, even under a spell; odds are good he's worth a lot of dollars.

We don't have the magic anymore, but she knows someone who does. As she pours me a glass of red—red, red, I'm fucking sick of red—I've finally found enough scraps to read between the lines.

"You're going to get the kids to hex Marty."

"I'm going to get them to use their power to help out a sister in need. Y'know, like we *used* to do."

"Annie, are you seriously going to turn those girls into murderers because of your marriage problems?"

Her eyes flash, and I realize too late the trap I've stepped into. "They're already murderers, Lori. Fierce little killers, just like us. Or didn't you hear about Dani's piece of shit stepdad?"

I didn't need to hear about it. I was there, close enough that his snapping neck was audible. Turns out it sounds a lot duller than I've been imagining all these years. And what she says just confirms what I already thought.

The girls killed Skeet.

He was a rotten asshole, and the way he died was mercifully quick for everyone, not just him. But the kids shouldn't have been

involved in it. A happy accident removes a guy like that from the world—like a boat of seal clubbers capsizing in the Arctic—you don't have to feel bad about it.

But four girls, not even out of school, get blood on their hands to make it happen? That's not right.

I'm only just realizing that we were all in the same boat when we were their age. Our parents were too high, too stupid, too self-obsessed or tired to give a shit. Belladonna was our appropriate adult and she didn't stop us, didn't protect us. She *enabled* us.

Now Anais is going to go one step further. She's going to point them at her husband like a loaded gun and use them to blow him away.

"So, you're going to convince them that he's an abusive fuck, is that it?"

"It has traction, don't you think? They've probably all had to watch someone beating on a person they love, never able to do something about it. I'm going to give them the chance to feel powerful. Righteous. They'll probably thank me for it."

"You're sick," I grunt.

"Yeah, Lori, I am. I'm sick and tired of having to pretend to be something I'm not. Sick of being the perfect wife, the Queen Bitch of this shithole of a town. Once I get that money, I'm out of here. I'm moving to Richmond like I should've years ago, before Marty convinced me we could have a life out here in the sticks."

"With us," I point out. "Your friends."

"Come with me," she says. I've finally stooped to drinking her wine, so when she says this I almost spit. "All of you. You, Elaine, Triss. It'll be just like old times, the four of us against the world. We'll have enough money to last us the rest of our lives."

I'm shaking my head before she even finishes. The idea of being with them like it was before sings to me like I'm Odysseus tied to a mast, but I can't trade those kids for that life. I'd never be able to forgive myself.

And I don't know what it says about Anais that she could.

"Think on it awhile. Please?"

"What happens if something goes wrong?" I ask. I know appealing to her conscience won't work, so maybe I can pick holes in her half-assed plan. "You heard Belladonna. The luck's run out. Sooner or later, it's going to catch up to us."

"You're just saying that because..." She trails off before the venom can leave her tongue, but I still feel it burn me.

Because you're dying.

She smiles sadly and puts a hand on mine. It might be real sympathy, but I just can't be sure anymore. I've seen her laughing and crying with barely a breath in between already today.

"They might be able to fix that for you too, Lori. Like we did before. They've got power, just like we used to. We should use it."

"Use *them*, you mean?"

Anais's pity curdles and she withdraws her hand, expression turning stony. She pulls a cigarette out of her purse and lights up. The smell of the smoke dries out my throat. I can feel another coughing fit coming on.

"You really think they're going to buy it? A black eye and a few tears?"

"You did. But maybe you're right. Maybe it's too...subtle for teenagers."

Before I can ask what she means, she jabs the cigarette into the back of her hand, twisting it like she's stubbing it in an ashtray. Her lips curl back as she bites down on the pain, but I can see the satisfaction flickering in her eyes as the ember dies.

"Annie..."

"You're right, Lori. It's bullshit, isn't it? Like a fucking soap opera. If we're going to do this, let's do it right. Let's build a narrative. You know all about that, don't you?"

She slams her other palm down on the bar between us and grabs an empty bottle, wringing its neck in her manicured and

pock-marked hand. She lifts the bottle like a hammer and smashes her own wrist until the bruise is fat and black and undeniable. I realize my mouth is open when a scattered fleck of wine stings my lips.

"Annie, you don't—"

The sound of breaking glass cuts me off, but it isn't the bottle. She's discarded it in favor of her wine glass, because it's finer and thinner and shatters more easily against the marble counter. All I can do is stare as she gouges the sharp edge into the side of her face and rips it across her cheek.

"Annie!"

"Who's going to want me now, Lori?!" she screams, bubbles popping at the corner of her crimson-slicked mouth. "That's what he asked me when he cut my fucking face. I can almost hear it in his voice. It's perfect."

She laughs as gore drips down her neck, soaking that sleek, fitted dress that always made her the object of desire and envy in equal measure. I'm rooted to the spot, staring at the wreckage of a woman who was once my best friend.

"Think I've got gauze in the medicine box. Need a shower. Change my clothes. I'll mop the floor later. He fired all the housekeepers when he moved into the fucking hotel, but if you want something done right, right?"

I say nothing. I'm dizzy from her madness. Nausea tightens in my throat. For a moment, all I can hear is the crackling in my lungs. All I can taste is bile.

"You can come with me if you want," Anais gurgles. She spits in my empty wine glass, same color as mine. "Or I can drop you in town."

"That's okay," I whisper. "I need a walk. Some fresh air."

She nods like she understands. "Clear your head. Feel better. Promise you'll think about what I said?"

"Sure," I lie.

I'm not going to think about it. I want to go back to the trailer park. I want to get stoned and forget about it all—Anais and the murder she's planning and the girls she's weaponizing and Christie, clinging to life in the hospital, and the fact that I'm dying a little bit more every day.

But I can't. In fact, I feel like I only have one option left. I have to go back to where it all started.

CHAPTER 23

MATRIARCH

I turn to the source. The one who knows. Who always knew.

I stare up at Belladonna's house and my heart feels even heavier than the tumors in my lungs. Maybe it was just the walk up here. I thought getting to Anais's place had been tough, but now I feel like I've climbed a mountain through the deep forest, with a wolf on my heels all the while. Still that feeling of being watched. Hunted.

I take as deep a breath as I can, hack up some blood, and climb the steps to the front door of the place I used to think of as my real home.

She opens the door before I knock. I find sympathy in her eyes. I could slip into it like an ocean and sink to the bottom. If she held her arms out, I'd fall against her chest and weep. If she told me everything would be okay, I'd believe her.

Instead, I square my shoulders and barge into her house like an ungrateful shit.

"I'm glad to see you, Loretta," she says, and her somber tone touches something inside me that makes me feel weak. How is

she still making me dance like this?

"Don't hear that too often these days."

"You're part of our family. You always will be. You and the others, you're like daughters to me."

"You feel that way about the new girls too?"

Belladonna pauses. I want to call it hesitation, but that might just be because I want a victory over her. The truth is, she holds all the cards and sees the whole board. I know being fierce changes nothing. She's going to drip feed me answers like she always has, leave me wanting more like the pills I use to keep the pain at bay.

I was an addict long before I started taking drugs.

"I'm glad they've found their way to the Craft. They're ambitious and smart and driven, but they lack guidance. We can give that to them. Isn't that what adults are for?"

"Maybe," I mutter.

My relationship with adults was never good. I split and left my parents in the trailer park first chance I got. If I'd followed their example, I'd have ended up a mom at 14, a meth addict by 16, or at least an alcoholic. They never noticed that boys weren't on the agenda, or the way I sickened at the mention of babies. Everything I ever wrote they referred to as "that shit".

One night, I came home from Christie's to find my dad had tossed all my notebooks in an oil drum to cook barbecue. I screamed and cried until I realized I was wasting my breath, so I wrote it all again and this time I hid it. I think that was when I realized I needed to hide *everything* from them.

They died before I ever made it big—he drove drunk and she overdosed—and all I felt was relief that they never got the chance to come around looking for money.

Belladonna was the closest thing to a mom I ever had. The only adult I'd ever connected with.

"It hurts me to see you like this, Loretta."

"Like what? This is all you. You did this to me."

She shakes her head sadly. "No. Don't say that."

"What, you disagree? Who offered me the magic? Who got me started mainlining hexes and rituals before I was even out of high school? Who taught me that a spell was the answer to all my problems? And who took the magic away again?"

"I didn't. Magic is a vital thing. It has a life all its own. And it has a lifespan. The magic runs out for all of us."

"Except you."

She lapses into silence again, picking and choosing the truths she will gift me. I'm getting sick of it. I decide to take control of the conversation.

"Something's following me. In the forest. I can feel it, breathing down my neck all the time. It has something to do with the magic, doesn't it?"

She doesn't answer, which means I'm not just imagining it. She stares at me and the sympathy in her eyes deepens. I want it to be real, but...

"Belladonna, what's going on? It's not as straightforward as the magic going away, is it? Something's coming for us. Me, Anais, Triss, Elaine. We worked up a debt and now it needs to be paid in full. Isn't that how it works?"

"Magic requires sacrifice."

I scoff. Yeah, I've learned that lesson. Every spell we ever worked, there was a sacrifice. We thought it began and ended with a rabbit, but we were fooling ourselves. Nothing was a victimless crime. Someone always got hurt. The people we deceived, the people we controlled, the people we cheated and swindled and left at the wayside. We left a trail of sacrifices to our own glory in our wake, and then we made little cuts on our palms to "pay the blood toll" so we could feel better about it all.

"We're the final sacrifices, aren't we? The offering that cancels all debts. Even yours."

Silence.

"How old are you, Belladonna?"

Silence.

"How many girls have you helped?"

Silence.

"How many rabbits?"

In the final, yawning gulf of nothingness she gives me, realization crystallizes with mounting horror. I see the pattern repeating over and over, going back I don't know how far. She doesn't need to answer my next question because I already know the truth.

"It's going to happen to the girls too, isn't it?"

"Not necessarily."

I don't grasp the meaning in those words. Does that mean it doesn't end like this for everyone? Is it only me the wolf's coming for? What did I do wrong?

"I can help, Loretta. If you let me. I can give you something that'll give you more time. Please, just...stay awhile. Have tea with me. Let me do something to ease your burden."

I want to. I want her to be Mom again. Right at that moment, I don't think I've wanted anything more.

Then I think about Christie and Courtney and the wolf, and how none of this would have happened without Belladonna in my life. "Fuck off, Bella."

Her expression doesn't change and her eyes don't harden, but I feel the temperature drop. Love chased out by the cold. She sighs. "You'd better go. You don't want to be outside after dark. Not in your condition."

I scowl at her and hobble out of her house. Those first few steps are the hardest. Once I clear the threshold, the walk home will be easy by comparison.

"I'm here if you change your mind," she says, twisting that knife in my back one last time.

I don't turn around, don't answer, don't acknowledge her.

I just go home. To the trailer park.

CHAPTER 24

A New Complaint

I'm walking back across Shady Acres, hand in hand with Jack Daniels, and he's lost weight since we hooked up at the liquor store. I think about how I helped cover up a murder a couple weeks back, and how I'll probably get away with it while Christie goes to jail for minor drug offenses, and I start laughing. So fucking absurd.

I don't even realize I'm being watched.

"Loretta?"

It's Courtney, wheeling her bike through the middle of the park. The sight of her sobers me a little. Equal chance the churning in my guts is vomit or guilt, ready to spew out all over the muddy ground.

"Heeey, Courtney!" I say, and wave. Trying to pretend I'm not drunk and failing. "Late for you to be out, ain't it?"

She shrugs. "Meemaw ain't making me go to school."

"Yeah, after what happened to your mom. Makes sense."

She stares at me and says nothing. I wonder how hurt Christie would be, seeing her daughter so angry, so resentful, that she

doesn't even see the point in staying home from school.

It's not even that, I realize. It's *indifference* I see in Courtney. Christie would hate it. Anger she could handle, but this? It'd drive her crazy.

"Going to see your friends? Mind if I walk with you?"

"It's a free country."

I laugh, high and sarcastic. I don't remember when I started to sound so bitter, but don't I have a responsibility to be honest with her? To give her a clear picture of the world she's growing up in? She's only free so long as no one else decides they know better, and only so long as she can pay for the privilege.

But if I tell her that, don't I have to admit the magic made everything easier? Right up until it didn't.

I glance at her, at the serious expression she's wearing. "Can I ask you a question?"

"Do I have to answer?"

"How about this? You answer my questions and I'll do the same for you."

She gives a nod, even if the look in her eye is skeptical. It's a good night to hold a Q&A like this. The air's muggy and stale, Confederate flags drooping, and the park's filled with a sticky heat that's chased everyone inside to their crappy desk fans and battered AC units. We're alone, save for the muted strains of bluegrass and the burble of whatever boxsets they're binging on shared Netflix passwords.

I like privacy.

"What do you want?" I ask. "From the magic?"

"I want to be happy," she says.

There's more to it than that. The ticking of her bike wheels is like the machinery of her mind turning her thoughts over. It has something to do with Christie, I figure, and maybe her friends. Maybe Dani. Their relationship whispered familiar.

But I asked and she answered, so... "Your turn."

"Were you in love with my mom?"

I snort. "Damn, girl. You don't mess around."

"Were you?"

"It's complicated."

It's always been complicated. I've tried putting it in words. Hell, the characters in my novels always seem to fall for the wrong people, and they always end up heartbroken. Some of them bounce back and find a purpose, some of them sink to the bottom of a bottle, but they never get the girl.

"I won't lie to you, Courtney. Other people are going to do that plenty. Yes, I was in love with your mom. I think I still am. There wasn't anything I wanted more than to be with Christie, except maybe the magic. When I realized I couldn't have both, I chose the magic."

"Do you regret it?"

"Nu uh, my turn! Where the fuck did Christie get those drugs?"

Courtney says nothing for a moment. When she speaks, her voice is hollow. "We found them. In an old church. Hidden under the floor."

I nod slowly. I remember. The church. Three dead bodies in shallow graves. Four girls helping us dig because Triss told them she'd introduce them to a genuine witch. Me, limping away with a handprint stinging on my cheek. Not one of my finest moments.

How many more secrets does that moldy dump have?

"Do you regret it?" Courtney asks again.

"Yes. Every single damn day. Maybe I didn't regret picking the magic—not at first—but I regretted what happened to Christie. I wished I'd been there for her, pulled her back from what she put herself through. I always thought it was unfair, that we'd all gotten what we wanted and she'd been left behind. Now I regret everything. All of it."

"Why?"

I don't bother enforcing the quid pro quo. My tongue is loose and limber, and I have no one else who wants to hear my stories anymore.

"We lost the magic, Courtney. No more hexes, no more charms, no more rituals. Those rabbit feet you girls are wearing now? Ours dried up like time was in fast forward. All the things we took for ourselves got taken back. Anais's marriage broke down on the quick, Elaine and Triss stopped being invisible to their neighbors, and...my cancer came back."

I feel a sense of satisfaction at the way she stiffens up. I want to tell her how it feels to have my body quit on me, to have the *magic* quit on me. Maybe I can scare her straight. Or maybe I'll just make things worse. If I try to steer her away, won't she just dig her heels in? Kids aren't stupid, but they're arrogant. They always assume they won't make the same mistakes, that they're smarter.

I know I did.

"This is where I'm going," Courtney says, snatching me back from my plan to set her right.

We're standing outside just another nondescript trailer, and I think maybe she's just trying to get me to leave, until I recognize the two girls peering through the blinds. The other two, Grace and Mary? Sisters. We never had that energy in our coven.

"You owe me an answer."

"How do you figure? You started."

"Because 'why' is still a question. But I'm not going to ask you anything. I just want you to think about something." I pause to make sure she's listening, but she's staring at me like there's nothing in the world but us. "Have a line. One you don't cross. Your magic's limited only by your imagination, so you need to decide how far you're going to take it, and don't take it any further than that. That was our problem, Courtney. We never had a line. I've done a lot of things I'm ashamed of. I don't want that for you. Any of you."

She leans her bike against the fence outside the trailer, silent as the grave. She walks up the steps, leaving me hanging on her answer.

"Night, Loretta," she mumbles, and slips inside. My heart plummets down to my knees.

Maybe she'll think about it. Maybe I lost her. Either way, I'm tired. I need to sleep, and I realize I wandered *way* past my own trailer walking with Courtney. I start the journey back, taking another slug from the bottle because my sorrows broke the surface.

I'm halfway home when I hear the growling, see something slinking between the trailers. Someone's guard dog maybe, only I don't remember seeing a dog that big in this neighborhood and shouldn't there be a fucking muzzle on that thing?

It's only when I stop to look and see it prowling between the mobile homes, straight toward me, that I realize it isn't a dog.

It's a wolf.

Black fur, red eyes, and the biggest fucking teeth I've ever seen on an animal, and it's staring right at me. Suddenly, I feel like a rabbit.

A jackrabbit.

I pitch the mostly empty bottle at the beast. It dodges—actually, it's more like it shifts aside the way a shadow would in the high beams of a passing car—and my missile thuds in the grass between the trailers. I'm sure I hear a hitch in its growling, like it's laughing at me. I've never been athletic.

Maybe that's why, when I start running, I feel like I'm moving through molasses back to my trailer, or maybe that's just the cancer crackling away in my lungs. I stop trying to breathe and focus on running. It occurs to me to scream for help, but I know better. I'd have more luck shouting *Fire!*, assuming I could speak.

Hope surges when I reach the front steps, and then I feel the jaws around my calf, the hot gush of blood on my foot. I scream as my skin tears like wet paper, and pry at the trailer door until it pops open. I tumble inside, weeping like a child, and kick the door shut on the monster's snout, listen to it scrabbling, trying to force its way in and devour me.

What comes next chills my blood, and I find myself praying that it's the booze, the drugs, the disease eating me alive from the inside, making me hallucinate.

I hear a man chuckling, hear the wolf walking away on two legs.

"Oh fuck..."

I limp in the direction of the bathroom for bandages and painkillers because the booze isn't cutting it. After the magic ran out, I thought it would be the cancer coming for me.

Turns out I was wrong.

CHAPTER 25

If It Makes You Happy

Mary and Grace are waiting for me in their trailer. Another tutoring session for Grace, who only seems to need to show up now to ace a test. Maybe even that's optional. Mary wraps her arms around me and squeezes. I guess she's used to playing big sister by now, but we haven't really spoken. None of us have.

And I still haven't heard from Dani.

Grace smiles shyly, like she's not sure what to say. She looks normal, not like someone who's helped kill a man and found a fortune, and whose own wish is coming rapidly true. For a moment, I think we all might be okay.

"Did you bring it?" she asks, eyeing my backpack.

"Bring what?" I ask, knowing full well what she means.

"The book."

There it is. From now on, it's always going to be about the book.

I shake my head.

"Told you she wouldn't." The sound of Dani's voice causes me to jump.

I hadn't expected her. "What are you doing here?" It sounds more like an accusation than I intend.

"Hanging out," she replies. She stares at me like a science project. It's hard to believe that only a few days ago, her lips were pressed to mine.

"You didn't call." I clear my throat, hoping to mask my disappointment.

"We thought..." Mary starts, "...it would be better to give you some time alone, in case you felt guilty."

I look from one face to the next. The conversation feels rehearsed. My mom is in the fucking hospital, and my friends are here, gossiping behind my back?

"Guilty about what?"

Dani steps closer and slides her arm around my waist. "About the spell. About what you did to Teeny."

My stomach churns. In all my shock and anger over the past couple of days, it didn't occur to me that this might be the result of my spell. I'd wished to be happy, and I thought the wish had come true when Dani and I spent the night together. But what if it hadn't? What if Teeny's overdose was my spell's way of trying to make me happy?

"Oh shit," Dani says, covering her mouth with her hand. "You didn't know."

My ears ring, and I fall back onto the couch.

I wake up on the bottom bunk of Mary and Grace's red metal bunk bed. Judging by the Pokémon sheets, I assume it's Grace's bed. The room looks mismatched, a combination of both the girls' personalities vomited onto the walls. It takes a moment for my mind to clear and for me to remember why I'm here.

I sit up and narrowly miss banging my head on the upper bunk.

Mary walks over and brushes my hair from my face. "You okay?"

I swallow the lump in my throat. "I'm sorry."

"It's okay," Mary says. "You can stay here if you want to. Our parents are out of town for a few days. My dad has a job interview."

I push myself off the bed. I have no idea how long I've slept. My throat is dry. "Could I have a glass of water?"

Mary nods and leads me into the kitchen. Dani and Grace sit at the table, leaning in and whispering conspiratorially. They straighten as Mary and I enter.

I take a seat beside Grace.

"I'm sorry, Court," Dani says, "I thought you already figured out about Teeny."

Maybe she did and maybe she didn't, but that didn't change the grin she tried to cover with her hand when she realized I hadn't known.

"Why were you asking about the book?" I glance at Grace, ignoring Dani for the moment.

"We need it to do another spell," Grace answers.

They're planning spells without me. I guess it makes sense. We've only just figured out the magic works, it's natural to plan the next steps. But Teeny's in the hospital, and they didn't even bother to call me. My thoughts tumble over one another. What if they think what happened to Teeny is a good thing, like with Skeet? No big deal, right? Just another dead junkie.

Mary places a glass of ice water in front of me and I down a few swallows before speaking again. "We just did a spell a few days ago, and if you haven't noticed, we're still living with the fallout. Why should we do another?" I can't hide the defensive tone.

It's Dani who answers. "To help Anais."

"The old witch?" I ask, and take another sip of water.

Dani nods.

"When did you... Why have you been talking to her?"

"Without me" are the words I want to add, but don't.

Dani's eyes narrow. "Her old man beat her up real bad. She wants our help to put him down, like we did Skeet."

My head hurts. There is something missing, something that the old witches are hiding from us. "Why does she need us? Aren't they supposed to be teaching us? Aren't they the powerful ones?"

Unless...

Loretta's words come rushing back to me. About losing the magic. I thought it was drunken rambling.

Mary takes a dish towel printed with roosters and wipes off the counter, watching.

"It's a powerful spell," Dani replies. "The rabbit ritual was a really powerful spell, too. You can't just do all that at one time, you know? It tapped them out, so they need us. We owe them."

"It doesn't make sense," I say. "We killed Skeet and found a shit-ton of drugs and cash. If magic worked like that, then *we'd* be tapped out, too. Loretta says their magic ran out. All the spells they've ever cast are coming undone."

Dani rolls her eyes. "Anais said she'd try to talk us out of it."

I cringe at the phrase "Anais said". "What do you mean?"

"Loretta has cancer, Court. They can't fix it. She's too far gone. Anais says she's mad about it, and if she can't use magic to fix it, she doesn't want anyone else to use magic either."

Somehow, I can't reconcile the two versions of Loretta competing for space in my head. One is a woman who loves Teeny, and seems worried about us, oddly enough. The other, a selfish woman who drove my mother to booze and drugs, and wants to take magic away from everyone else.

I take another sip of water, trying to put it together in my brain like a jigsaw puzzle I don't have all the pieces for. More immediate than my worries about Loretta and Anais is the nagging question in the back of my mind: Did my spell put Teeny in the hospital?

CHAPTER 26

So Much for Sisterhood

Anais's house is a crude mockery of Belladonna's, but what it lacks in charm, it makes up for in size. We abandon our bikes in the driveway beside a pair of luxury SUVs.

Dani pushes open the heavy oak door, not bothering to knock. It's only been a couple of days, but still, I wonder how many times she's been here. She leads us into the kitchen, where Triss and Elaine are sipping glasses of wine. An empty bottle sits between them. They aren't on their first glass.

I search the room for signs of Loretta. Despite Anais's words to Dani, and Meemaw's warnings, her presence would be a comfort. She's one of the few adults who seems to give a shit about us, who doesn't just look at us and write us off as trash or useless, or both. It's funny; if Meemaw didn't hate her so much, they'd probably get along.

"You okay, Court?" Grace's hand slips into mine. I smile at her, trying to reassure her, displaying confidence I don't feel.

"Yeah."

Triss walks to the cabinet and pulls out four more wine glasses. "You girls want a drink?"

The "yes" is out of Dani's mouth before I can refuse.

"Where's Loretta?" I ask, as Triss flutters around, passing out the glasses. Underage drinking must be what passes for bonding in her eyes.

"She won't be joining us." Triss favors Dani with a smile. "She turned on us. Didn't Dani tell you?"

Grace squeezes my hand. "I thought you said covens are family?"

Elaine waves Grace's concern away. "It's a little spat. That happens with sisters. I'm sure we'll all be back together again before you know it, laughing at our silly little disagreement."

It might be true, but something still bothers me. "Will the magic still work if she isn't here? Don't you need four?"

That's what Triss told me in the churchyard: *There must always be four*.

Triss turns and overbalances, placing a hand on the bar to steady herself. Forget first glass, that probably wasn't their first bottle of wine. "Anais has come up with something *special*."

I hate the way she lingers on the word, and the way I shrink beneath the weight of her stare. I study the intricately carved molding that runs along the edges of the bar to avoid meeting her eyes.

"What about the other lady?" Grace asks. I could hug her. She's never been brave, and I wonder if she also senses that something isn't right.

"Belladonna?"

I jump at the sound of Anais's voice behind me. Dani told me her husband hurt her, but I wasn't ready for the reality. He didn't just hit her; he slashed her face. I can see blood and puss oozing from under the gauze, and I swallow the bile rising in the back of my throat.

"She doesn't trouble herself over these little, *trivial* things."

It's a person's life. The life of a man she's been married to maybe as long as I've been alive. But killing him is *trivial*? Is that what the rabbit ritual did to them? What it will do to us?

Dani turns up her glass and we fall in line behind Anais as she leads us out the back door and onto the deck surrounding her pool.

"The drainage out here is better," she explains. "It makes for an easier cleanup."

"Cleanup?" Mary asks, setting her still-full glass on a wicker table that costs more than all the furniture in Meemaw's trailer combined. "Don't we just need a burnt piece of paper and a personal item? That's what we did for Skeet."

The area around the pool is concrete and terracotta-colored tile, with a few small drains scattered around. Centered over one of the drains is something tall, covered with a white cloth. Anais tugs the cover off with a flourish.

"Ta-da!" she sings, as we glimpse two majestic, white doves in a wrought iron cage.

"What do we have to do?" Grace asks. Her voice trembles.

Anais offers two pairs of thick gardening gloves, giving one pair to me and the other to Dani. "Each of you take one of the birds."

Dani doesn't hesitate. She slides her hand in the glove and reaches into the cage, pulling out a writhing dove.

Anais hands Mary a long blade, so thin it might have been a needle. "Pierce its heart."

Mary glances over her shoulder at me.

"Do it!" Dani snaps.

Mary's hands shake, and she thrusts the skinny blade into the dove's breast, red drips onto the white feathers, staining them. The bird stills. We've taken another life.

"Now you," Anais says, looking at me.

I reach into the cage and gently wrap my hands around the remaining bird. Its tiny heart hammers against the fabric of the glove. My eyes sting.

Anais passes the needle-like blade to Grace, who stares at

me, eyes wide with horror.

"Does she have to?" Mary asks, her voice thick with emotion.

"You all have to play a part," Triss answers. "It gets easier. Trust me."

But I don't want it to get easier to kill.

Grace stands frozen in horror, knife poised.

"Don't be such a baby, Grace," Dani says, not bothering to mask her sneer.

A tear rolls down Grace's cheek, and before she can move, I thrust my hand into the air, releasing my grip on the bird. The tension loosens from Grace and Mary's shoulders as the dove spreads its wings and vanishes into the forest. The tears fall freely down my cheeks.

"What the fuck are you doing, Court?" Dani demands.

Her hands grip my shoulders. She shakes me so hard my teeth clatter together. I want to shove her off, I want to explain myself, but all I can do is stand there and cry.

"Let her go!" Grace yells, a sound I haven't heard before. She grabs Dani's arm and pulls her off me. Dani growls as she spins and shoves Grace onto the hard concrete below.

Something in me wakes up. I grab Dani's shoulder and spin her around. I feel the sting of the slap against my open palm before I realize I've struck her.

Dani blinks; it's her turn to be in shock.

"It's okay, honey." Sensing the show is over, Anais creeps in and puts an arm around Dani's shoulder. "They aren't ready."

"I told you, we should've done this inside," Triss says. "Which bird got away?"

"Loretta's," Anais answers. "But never mind that now. Why don't we get this cleaned up? Would you girls like to go for a swim? The pool is heated."

She strokes Dani's hair and her livid expression softens.

"What the fuck is wrong with all of you?" I don't recognize the sound of my own voice. "You just kill people and animals like

it doesn't matter as long as you get what you want. Teeny was right. You're *monsters*."

Anais laughs, and she actually sounds amused. "Teeny? You want to talk about your mom? How about this? She had bigger dreams than any of us, and she was smart. So very, fucking smart. She wanted out of Shady Acres so bad, and she thought she had it all figured out. She could have had *anything* she wanted if she'd just followed through, but she couldn't. She *betrayed* us. Our coven almost fell apart when she turned her back on us, all because of one, stinking rabbit. If Elaine hadn't stepped up..."

"What?" I ask, but I don't want to know. "What would have happened?"

"We would have lost everything," Anais answers, an angry glint in her eye. "It wasn't just her life on the line. It was *all of ours* and she nearly ruined everything, all because she decided a ball of fur was more important than her friends. You ask me, she deserved everything she got."

"You hexed her?"

Anais smirks, tightening her grip around Dani's shoulder. "Oh, we didn't need to. She crumbled like a sandcastle the first time someone offered her a needle. I'm surprised it's taken her this long to kill herself, honestly. Besides, you're one to talk. You cast the spell that helped her along. Hell, you even gave her the drugs to do herself in with."

One look at Dani and I know she's told Anais everything. Of course she fucking has.

"I'm done," I say.

I don't trust my legs. My whole body trembles, but somehow, I put one foot in front of the other and leave them all standing around the pool and the empty cage.

I've barely made it back to my bike when their words finally register.

Which bird got away?

Loretta's.

So much for sisterhood.

CHAPTER 27

GOT ME WRONG

COURTNEY

Mary and Grace aren't on the bus, and when Mary doesn't show for third period—US History—I start to worry. We haven't spoken since the broken ritual at Anais's house.

At lunch, I sit alone at our usual table in the corner and unwrap my bag—bologna and cheese on wheat bread, a juice box, an orange, and a baggie of goldfish crackers. I peel the crusts off the bread and chew, keeping an eye out for Heather, or any of my other tormentors. Mary and I sit together mostly out of habit, but also because there's safety in numbers. It was more effective when we had Dani too.

It's my first day back at school since Teeny's overdose, and people are giving me a wide berth, as if tragedy is somehow contagious. *Fuck 'em*, I think, but the thought sounds like Dani's voice in my head, and that hurts. I can feel the burning threat of tears, and I don't want to walk around red-nosed and puffy-faced for all these assholes to think I'm upset over Teeny.

Fuck 'em. This time it sounds like Meemaw's voice, and I smile.

"Hey, trailer trash!"

I don't lift my head. I don't look over. I recognize Heather's voice.

"I'm speaking to you, short bus." Her hand slams down on the table, and I jump despite myself.

As if I don't have enough shit to deal with.

"What do you want?"

"Your dipshit brother seriously damaged my car. You owe me."

I roll my eyes. "Maybe if you weren't such a bitch people wouldn't throw rocks at your car."

She grabs the sandwich from my hand and tosses it onto the floor, stomping it with her designer boot.

"Seriously?" I ask.

"You thought licking my car was bad?" She leans close, sensing my weakness. In my loneliness, I make an easy target for her. "You're going to eat that off the floor."

She thinks she can break me. I'm alone, with my friends nowhere to be found, and my druggie mother half dead in the hospital. Heather underestimates me.

My face burns, but not with shame this time.

I catch her by a fistful of hair, and as her eyes go wide with shock, I slam her face down into the table. Hard.

She comes back up, blood gushing from her newly crooked nose. "You bitch!"

I stand and sweep a leg under her, knocking her to the floor. All the anger and hurt and embarrassment she's heaped at my feet since elementary school finally erupts.

"You fucking eat it!" I shout, grabbing the ruined sandwich. I straddle her, and rub the bread in her face, smearing her with blood and mustard.

The noise of chatting and chewing has quieted, people stand and squeeze in closer to get a better look, pulling out phones and

scrambling to take a video. Courtney Fowler has finally snapped.

Heather's once perfect face is already starting to swell. Even beneath the caked-on bits of sandwich and gushing blood, it looks bad. I'd feel worse if she hadn't spent every waking moment of her free time tormenting me.

Hands tighten under my arms and pull me off Heather. She's crying and I'm screaming, and the sounds mingle to take up the entire space of the cafeteria.

"I hope it hurts, you fucking bitch." I kick at her again but miss. "Good luck getting Daddy to pay for another nose job!"

Mr. Hensley, history teacher and boy's baseball coach, turns me around. "Vice Principal's office, Courtney." His voice isn't angry. Plenty of his players are from Shady Acres. He glances at Ms. Wallace who has appeared from the other side of the room, then down at Heather. "Get her to the nurse."

After a short march down the hallway, past the rows of faded blue lockers, trailed by the eyes of every asshole in the school, Mr. Hensley deposits me outside the Vice Principal's office. If I'm lucky, my behavior will be chalked up to "trouble at home" and I'll get off easy.

But when have things ever been easy for me?

Half an hour and a sign up for mandatory sessions with the school counselor later, I'm dismissed from school for the rest of the day. He doesn't say the word suspension when he calls Meemaw to come and pick me up, but it doesn't stop the long, silent looks in the rearview mirror on the way home.

"Courtney," Meemaw begins, "you know—"

"I'm fine," I snap. "There is no hidden meaning here. I'm not covering up grief or pain or whatever people think I'm bottling up. Heather has picked on me since elementary school, when she started a rumor that I didn't brush my teeth. She's an asshole, and she ruined my lunch."

"So, you're telling me you picked a fight because you're *hangry*?"

Something about hearing Meemaw use the word "hangry" strikes me as hilarious, and I laugh.

"Guess we'd better *yeet* ourselves over to the nearest McDonalds then."

"Oh, God, please stop."

Despite my words, I'm laughing so hard she has to order for me when she pulls into the drive-thru.

The smell of deep-fried potatoes fills Meemaw's ancient station wagon. She could've given me a hard time about the fight, but she didn't, just like she never gave Teeny a hard time about her problems. Somehow, I feel like both of us have failed her.

"Meemaw?" I ask, pulling a fry from the bag. It's so hot, it burns my fingertips. I pop it into my mouth, puffing out air around it as I swallow.

"Yeah, baby?"

"Do you remember telling me about when Teeny was young, and those girls she used to hang out with?" I'm pretty sure the French fry has permanently scorched the roof of my mouth.

"Mmhm."

"I met them." The confession feels good. "Not just Loretta, all of them. You remember the house you sent me to clean for that lady, Belladonna? She's like their ringleader or something."

Meemaw purses her lips. "I see."

"They wanted us to help them with some stuff, and at first it seemed okay, but now it's not. And, well, Dani... I think she wants to be like them. It's like she's changed."

What I don't say, but increasingly fear, is that maybe Dani *hasn't* changed. Maybe this is who she's been all along, but then I remember the time in sixth grade when Heather threw my library books into a storm drain. In retaliation, Dani stole the tires from Heather's bike. Twice.

Meemaw rummages around in the bag for her cheeseburger and hands it to me. "Open this for me, would you?"

I unwrap the wax paper and hand it back.

"Thanks." She chews in silence, and I'm not sure if she's waiting on me to say more, but I don't. I don't know what else *to* say.

By the time we turn into Shady Acres, we've polished off two cheeseburgers, a large order of fries, and two milkshakes.

I collect the empty wrappers and Meemaw waves me into the trailer.

The screen door screeches shut behind me, and I wonder absently if I should spray it down with WD40. Inside, Meemaw vanishes down the hall, and in a few minutes, I hear her rustling in the back closet.

She returns to the living room carrying a large cardboard box and drops it at my feet.

"What's this?" I lift one of the side flaps to reveal notebooks with neon rainbow dolphins and horses on the overs. I recognize the patterns—Lisa Frank.

"These are your mom's. She used to scribble in them all the time. She was going to be a songwriter, so she kept journals."

"You've read them?" I ask.

She shakes her head. "I didn't need to, but maybe you do. Might be something in there could help you."

I carry the box to my room and hit play on the boombox. Courtney Love's voice rings out as, one by one, I open the notebooks and read through them. They contain song lyrics and poems about whichever boys or girls she fancied that week. Later entries are notes that look like spells. I guess it makes sense, she was originally part of the coven, but it's weird to have the evidence in front of me.

The more straightforward "Dear Diary" notes mention Loretta, Anais, Triss and sometimes Elaine, in varying amounts of detail. There are pages and pages dedicated to Jake Washburn.

Teeny said she knew Heather's dad. She wasn't bluffing. In places, the text reads like the start of an enemies-to-lovers romance novel. It's clear he'd been in love with Teeny.

I wonder if Heather knows, if that's why she hates me.

Anais and the others are wrong. Teeny didn't part ways with them because she'd been weak. She was strong. There'd been a line she wasn't willing to cross; Teeny wouldn't harm others for her own gain. She thought Loretta wouldn't cross it either. She was heartbroken when Loretta proved her wrong.

I reach for the rabbit's foot charm. I've been an idiot. The warning signs were all there, but I trudged forward, regardless of the risks to me, Dani, Mary and Grace. I lift the charm from my neck and roll up the cord, pressing it against my nose and inhaling the musky scent of the fur one last time. I tuck it, and one of Teeny's notebooks, in the top drawer of my dresser.

Meemaw is on the sofa with her knitting when I finally emerge. "You okay?" she asks.

"Will you take me to see her?"

She nods. I don't have to say who I mean.

CHAPTER 28

It Has to End This Way

Belladonna's home looks like a tombstone draped in ivy. I carved an epitaph for myself here years ago, but I'm only just beginning to be able to read it.

Here lies Loretta Dandridge. Sucker.

It's a long walk from where the bus quits and heads back to town, but thanks to the pill bottle I emptied this morning, I can't remember most of the journey. The lost time doesn't concern me; it's more like lost pain at this point anyway.

I climb the steps to the veranda. Cold slices across the back of my legs and arms. The scarf helps, and I've started wearing a beanie to keep the heat in where my hair used to be. No one's sitting outside today, but I wonder if, once the weather warms up, Belladonna will bring the girls lemonade while they plan their next ritual. And if she'll bring them wine in a few years, once they have everything they want and nothing they need.

I don't know if I'm welcome in the house anymore, but I'm not a vampire—not dead yet—and I don't need anyone's permission to enter. In a fit of rebellion, I don't even knock. Fuck it.

I hear someone laughing in the parlor where they killed the rabbit. I recognize it as the giddy glee of the newly powerful. Someone talking with Belladonna and Anais, who's regaling them with tales of the old days. I hear them embellishing stories of the things I count among my greatest regrets.

Through the door, I flick a glance to the three of them, thick as thieves, wedged into the old sofa, joined at the hip, all smiling. Dani, but where's her coven? I wonder why she's here and the others aren't.

I go to the kitchen. No one challenges me. If they did, I don't know what I'd tell them. Why am I here? What am I hoping for? To catch one of the girls alone so I can put the fear into them, make them stare into my hollow eyes and my bloody lips for a glimpse of their future? Maybe to find the *Book of Shadows* lying around unattended so I can slip it under my sweater and into the oil drum fire outside my trailer, and my neighbors can light their joints on the flames of the witch book that ruined my life?

Neither of those long shots come good, and I find myself in the kitchen with Triss and Elaine. They're hissing at each other, glaring daggers, but they fall silent when they see me, argument forgotten in the heat of their mutual enmity for the woman who exposed the sham of their marriage.

"I'll talk to Belladonna," Triss says, and hefts a wine bottle from the rack.

She pecks Elaine on the cheek. She leans in, eyes fluttering closed, hoping for more, but Triss is already sweeping out of the room, shooting me a killing look as she passes.

Well, good luck, bitch. Dead woman walking here.

"Why are you here?" Elaine asks, once Triss is gone.

Her voice is quiet, timid, and lacks judgment. She was always the youngest, mousiest of the group. The boldest thing she ever did was hexing Triss in love with her, and after that all she wanted was to be left alone.

I always felt closer to Anais or Triss—we had fierceness in common—but Elaine's the only one who hasn't hurt me recently. I'm actually willing to answer the question.

"Don't really know. People used to want me around here."

"We still want you here, Lori," she says, and the sincerity in her voice makes my sore heart ache. "You're our friend. That didn't change. We just...wish you weren't so angry at us."

I sigh. "Fucking...goddamn it, Elaine..."

"Sorry. I didn't mean to upset you."

I pinch my nose, propping my weary bones against the counter. Elaine pours me a glass of crystal-clear water from the faucet and sets it in front of me, like I can use it to wash the mud out of my brain.

"You and Triss okay?" I ask, belatedly. I'd have thought I had no right to ask, but Elaine seems to think we're still friends.

She shakes her head. "We're fighting a lot. About everything. I snore and hog the covers at night. She never liked my cooking. She's getting sick of my dad talking about how the queers and Blacks ruined this town. I think I never realized how much we needed that hex. I thought she could love me for me, that I was enough. Guess I was fooling myself."

"We were all fooling ourselves." I drain half the glass of water. Even that's enough to make me feel bloated, diluted. "Are you... splitting?"

Another shake of her dainty head. "Like she says, love is a choice. And once we get the feet and the magic comes back, we'll..."

She claps her hands over her mouth. Apparently, that's a secret I shouldn't know, even if we are still friends.

"What do you mean 'once you get the feet?'"

"I shouldn't—"

"Elaine, what's happening? What are you guys planning?"

Last I heard, Anais had it all figured out—the girls, her husband, an escape plan, all of it. And it seemed like it was all going her way, since I read Marty's obituary a few days back, and got Anais's invitation to the service yesterday.

Was it yesterday? What day even is it?

Now it seems like maybe the plan has changed.

"Belladonna says it'll work," she blurts, like she's been holding it in so long her pressure gauge is redlining. "If we get the feet, we'll have the magic back. The girls have worn them long enough. They've already taken two lives. They're strong, Lori. Maybe stronger than we ever were, but..."

"So what happens to them?"

"We *need* this. Me and Triss. We talked about it and...we want it. Both of us. We want to be in love again, perfect again. If we have the feet, it'll work. Love is a choice, Lori, and we're choosing love."

"What's going to happen to those fucking kids, Elaine?!"

"The Wolf'll come for them. That's the deal. Four rabbits for power. Four rabbits for survival. It's them or us. Literally, it's them or us."

The sun winks out in that moment, and for achingly long seconds, it's me and Elaine under a single spotlight, in a singularity of that moment, everything else in shadow. What she has said sinks in slowly, filtering through the dead cells infesting my body and the aggregate of dissolved pills, to a place of understanding.

I've been a bigger idiot than I thought these past twenty years. When Belladonna said the rabbit ritual was a sacrifice, I'd always assumed she meant the animal.

She didn't. She meant us. We were committing to *being* sacrificed.

Four rabbits.

"Lori..."

"No... You can't... Elaine, are you..."

"Lori."

"They're kids, Elaine! You're talking about sacrificing *children*. And for what? A loveless marriage? Money? Are you fucking crazy?!"

"Lori, you're hurting me!"

I pull my hands off her wrists. I didn't even realize I'd grabbed her. Her blood's curled up under my fingernails. She weeps. Blood and tears, she weeps.

"Y-you can't stop us," she sobs. "We're doing this. Anais is going to talk to Dani, tonight. She's going to get her to bring us the feet. She thinks she's going to join us. *Our* coven. But it doesn't have to be her. It can still be you. I..." Her voice breaks, and now she's full-on crying. Saline drips off her chin and spots the sweater she's wearing over her dress. "I *want* it to be you. Like before."

"This is insane," I tell her, and the words feel right in my mouth. They taste like truth. "We built our own hell, Elaine. We were so angry about the world fucking us, we didn't realize we were just fucking ourselves. This was a card tower; it was all going to fall down eventually. We need to shut up and take our medicine."

"I don't want to die."

"*Neither do I!*"

I stun her into silence with that. The anger, the terror, that comes out of me surprises even me. But it's how strong, how level I sound that really gets me.

I *don't* want to die. But I'm going to. And I'm not putting anyone else in the grave in my place.

Fuck that.

"We can't do this," I affirm.

"We don't have a choice," someone says.

Triss, speaking for Elaine, as she's done so many times before. They've always complemented one another so well, sometimes I forgot it was all bullshit. Kinda wish they'd throw this kind of effort into marriage counseling instead. Then maybe they'd stand a chance.

She stands between me and the parlor, arms folded, and I try to forget that I saw her murder three men with a baseball bat.

"Out of my way, Triss. I'm not playing."

"Neither am I, Lori. This is happening, whether you like it or not. Dani's already gone. Anais is driving her home right now."

My guts heave when I realize I'm too late. The feeling only gets worse when Triss still doesn't move. I know what they're planning, and like an idiot, I told them I wouldn't stand for it. Which means they can't just let me go.

"I'm sorry, Loretta," Belladonna says, swishing in from the parlor like a ghost in a flowing, white dress.

I wonder how long she's haunted this old house. I wonder how many other covens there have been, how many other rabbits she's sacrificed. She might have killed even more people than us.

What's one more?

She looks at me, woe in her eyes, and takes my bony hand in hers. "I'm sorry it has to end this way."

CHAPTER 29

RECYCLED DREAMS

COURTNEY

It's weird to see Teeny just lying there in the hospital bed, hooked up to God knows what machines. Almost everything in the room is white. White walls, white sheets, white blankets, so much goddamned white. It smells like the inside of a disinfectant bottle.

Guilt stabs my gut like a serrated knife, jagged and messy. Did my spell do this? Just when I convince myself it isn't my fault, I think of another ten reasons why it is.

Meemaw squeezes my hand. "You sure you don't want me to stay?"

"Yeah. I'll be okay." It's hard to say whether or not that's the truth. "Besides, you should be there when Freddie gets home."

The *real* truth is, I want to be done with magic, but I don't know what will happen if I reject the coven. Will it undo our spells and fix Teeny? Will the others replace me, like the older women did with my mom? At this point, I think Dani would, but after the broken ritual, Mary and Grace might hesitate. Besides, I still have the book.

An uncomfortable thought forms in the back of my mind: *If the book was so important, why would Belladonna let me find it?*

I have too many unanswered questions about the older coven. The easiest answer is that Loretta is probably telling the truth. The magic is gone, and they want to use us to do things like kill their husbands for them, but something about that theory doesn't quite work, and I can't figure out what. Did they lose their magic over time, with age? Or is it because they misused it? Is magic finite?

I've heard of the rule of three, but these older witches don't concern themselves with it. Maybe I owe Loretta a visit.

I drag a pink upholstered chair—the only thing in the room that isn't white—over beside Teeny's bed and take her hand. "I read your diaries," I start, settling into the chair. "I should've asked you about the coven. I shouldn't've just believed what they said about you."

Teeny lies there, pale and silent, looking more like a corpse than an angel. The machines surrounding her make rhythmic beeping noises.

"I'm sorry about what they did to you." Pressure builds behind my eyes. "With friends like those, who needs enemies, right? But I'm worried. They've got Dani, and what if it's too late to help her? I love her." I realize it's the first time I've ever said it out loud. "When you wake up, I think we should talk about it."

I open my bag, taking out a book of stories to read to her while she sleeps. I flip through the table of contents. There's Poe, Lovecraft, Jackson, all the names I expect.

I clear my throat and begin with *The Tell-Tale Heart*. By the time I've made it to *The Lottery*, there's a nurse standing in the doorway, hesitantly.

"Reading to her?"

I bite back a sarcastic comment about stating the obvious.

"She can hear you, you know," the nurse says, crossing the

room and checking the monitors. "Some people think they can't when they're out like this, but I've seen people wake up and remember whole conversations that happened while they were asleep."

"Really?"

"Really." She checks the bag hanging from Teeny's IV.

"Is she going to be okay?" I ask. I can hear the break in my voice. My mouth is too dry to swallow.

Keep it together, Courtney.

"Is she your mom?" the nurse asks.

I can't risk speaking again, so I nod.

"She's going to be okay, darlin'. She just needs to rest up and get all the junk out of her system. She came in malnourished and dehydrated. By the time she leaves here, she'll be good as new." She places a gentle hand on my shoulder, then exits, leaving me alone with Teeny, and my grief.

When I'm sure she's gone, I clear my throat. "It sucks to be judged by somebody who doesn't know you. And I don't...know you. I thought I knew, but I'm an idiot. I got so mad at you for not being perfect that I forgot you're just a person. Reading your journals... You were amazing. You lost so much."

I pause and inhale slowly. The weight of guilt, anger and fear have pressed down on me for so long they feel like a security blanket. It's hard to let them go.

"I don't think I've ever asked you for anything, at least not much, but I'm asking you to be better. I want to be better too. We can do it together. I promise I won't give you a hard time when you fuck up."

My breath hitches in my throat.

"I love Meemaw, but there's stuff I can't talk to her about. I need you, Mom."

Teeny's eyelids flutter. It might be something or it might be nothing. I scoot the chair closer and lay my head beside hers, sweeping her damp, sweat-soaked hair off her forehead.

"Some of your songs and poems were really good." I sniffle and wipe the tears rolling down my cheek before they reach her pillow. "I'm sorry you didn't get to live your dreams, but maybe we can make new dreams."

I consider calling Meemaw to pick me up when I finally leave the hospital, but I feel like walking. I'm not ready to go home yet. I'm not ready to think about going back to school tomorrow, and wonder whether Heather will be there, all bruised and swollen. I'm sure she knows about her dad and Teeny. Maybe that's why she hates me; it's genetic.

Instead of going home to face my thoughts, I head into the woods.

CHAPTER 30

Chickens Coming Home to Roost

We haven't used the church much since we found the drug stash. The floor has collected a new layer of detritus. I press my face against the cool stone of the crumbling wall.

"Courtney?" Grace's voice cuts through the silence.

"Yeah." I run a hand through my hair. "What are you doing here?"

She smiles, a nervous and fleeting thing. It's only been a few days, but, even more than the others, I've missed her innocence. "We didn't go to school today."

"I noticed." I tilt my head to indicate the place beside her. "Can I sit?"

"Oh! Yeah!" She scoots over and I fill the empty space.

"Where's Mary?"

"She went to see Dani." Grace squirms and looks as uncomfortable as I feel. "It isn't what you think, though. She's not sneaking around. She's glad you did what you did."

I nod and swallow the lump in my throat. "Then why are you guys avoiding me?"

"Mary's embarrassed. She said she should've done what you did."

"It was hard," I say. "With the older witches watching. And Dani. When it feels like the whole world wants you to do something, not doing it isn't easy."

Grace nods and presses against me. I put an arm over her shoulder, something I'd seen Dani do hundreds of times. I hope it's a comfort.

"So, what is she doing then?" I ask. Part of me hopes she's trying to bring Dani to her senses, to tell her we've gone too far.

"She's giving back our rabbit feet."

It takes a few seconds to process the words. "Why?"

"Dani came to our house," Grace explains. "She was yelling and cussing, and Mom threatened to call the cops, so Mary said she'd meet her in the woods and told me to wait here."

It's like a punch to the gut. Why would Dani go to their house and cause a scene? "What about the coven?" I ask.

Grace shrugs. "We can't be part of it when we move anyway." She sounds resigned, but this is news to me.

"When you move?"

"Daddy got a job at some big tech company." Her voices shakes. "Mom says we're moving out of Shady Acres. We're going to California."

I pull her in tight for a hug. She's on the verge of tears.

"I'm going to miss you, Courtney."

"I'll miss you, too. I'm sorry I failed at tutoring you." It's a silly thing to say, but I can't think of anything else.

"It's okay. I got an A on my last test anyway. Do you think the spells will last, even if we leave? I don't want my grades to suck again."

I brush her reddish-blond hair over her shoulder. "I'm not sure what will happen." But I think, maybe, we shouldn't use magic if we can help it. At least, not the kind we've *been* using.

I'm glad we got the chance to be closer, but I wish I'd never found that stupid fucking book." I sit with my arm around her until Mary arrives.

She doesn't look me in the eye. "Hey."

"Grace says you're moving."

"Yeah."

"Were you even going to tell me?" I search her face. When her lip shapes a frown, it's all the answer I need.

"Right." I stand and brush dirt and leaf matter from my legs. "Bye then."

When I walk past, she grabs my wrist. "Court?"

"What?" I barely resist the urge to roll my eyes.

"Be careful with Dani." Her grip is so tight, her knuckles turn white. I try to yank free, but she keeps hold, pulling me in close to whisper. "Seriously, she's snapped. She was threatening to come after us if I didn't give her the rabbit's feet."

"Come after you how?"

Mary lifts her shoulder and gives a worried frown. "I didn't ask. I just gave her what she wanted. We're leaving anyway, and I don't want her near Grace. She's majorly pissed off about what went down at Anais's house. She's still been going over there. Watch your back, okay?"

I nod and place my hand over hers.

As I leave the church and head back toward home, I wonder if that's the last time I'll see Grace and Mary. I wonder what will become of our coven, of our church.

The sun's about to set when I arrive at Meemaw's trailer. Dani's bike leans against the side of the porch. I take a deep breath and push the door open.

Meemaw is in her usual spot with her knitting bag at her feet.

Based on the color of the yarn, I suspect she's knitting something for me. She nods to a small box on the coffee table. "Someone left that for you at the door."

I lift the wooden box. The latch is secured with a white ribbon and a tag with my name written in calligraphy. I flip the tag, searching for the name of whoever left it, finding nothing. It's surprisingly lightweight.

"Do you know who left it?" I ask.

She shakes her head. "Didn't see nobody."

My instinct tells me that maybe it was Loretta. Who else would leave it without a name?

"Dani's in your room," Meemaw says.

"Thanks."

After what Mary said, I'm not surprised Dani's here. I tuck the box under my arm and head down the hallway, my heart pounding out a quick rhythm in my chest. I push open my door and peer in, wordlessly.

Dani has her back to the door. My backpack is on the bed, and she's rummaging through it. I think back to Mary's warning.

Dani isn't here to see me.

"It isn't in there," I say.

She jumps and turns, her face full of panic for two seconds before she remembers to put on her mask of calm collectedness. "What isn't?"

Of all the options she could've went with, playing dumb isn't the one I would've guessed. I step into the room and place the box on my bedside table.

"The book." I fold my arms across my chest. "That's why you're here, isn't it?"

"No, Courtney, of course not." She crosses the room and takes my hands in hers. "I didn't know when you'd be back. I was looking for a notebook and a pen so I could leave you a note."

I want to believe her. I want so desperately to believe her. Her eyes are wide and bright, and she stands straighter, like someone unencumbered by the weight of an abusive stepfather, or the murder of two people. Is this what she would've been like if her life had been different? Is this what happiness is for Dani?

I've seen her angry, scared, frustrated, but I can't say whether or not I've seen her truly happy. Her smile is a dull ache in my stomach because I know what caused it. Power. Death.

She brushes my bangs off my forehead. "I've missed you."

I glance at the carpet. I don't trust myself to meet her eyes. "I'm not the one that's been avoiding you," I counter.

"You slapped me." She extends her lower lip into a pout, which is as infuriating as it is adorable.

"You shoved Grace," I say.

"Because she grabbed me," Dani says. "It was a reflex. I didn't mean to. *And* I wasn't avoiding you. You know I don't do well with...stuff. And it's been a lot. Skeet and Mom, and Teeny."

"You had time for Anais and her cronies." I hate how petulant I sound.

"They don't know me like you do." She places her hand on my shoulder, stroking my collarbone. "They didn't give me their milk at recess in third grade because I dumped mine in Heather's lap for calling you 'Food Stamp'. Didn't take the blame when we got caught shoplifting lipstick from CVS. Didn't save me from Skeet. That was all you."

Her fingers dance across my skin, making me tingle. We could've been happy. Maybe we still can. I tilt my head and kiss her hand.

She strokes my cheek.

My whole life I've had a recurring dream that I'm stranded in the middle of the ocean, treading water, surrounded by nothing for miles around. Every stroke is a struggle to stay above water, and no matter how hard I try, I know it's only a matter of time.

It's how I feel now. My body ignores the protests of my mind and responds to her touch. I lean in for her lips.

CHAPTER 31

CHOICES

Triss and Elaine's success never came from magic like mine. It came from hard work and dedication. That's why they still drive a Lexus. The interior's leather, which is good because my blood will wipe off.

I come around with my face stuck to the backseat. The cut on my brow turns half my vision red. I try to scrub my eye with my scarf and realize someone's tied my hands. Probably Triss. I can't imagine Elaine restraining anyone.

I try to sit up and everything occurs to me at once, with a clarity I haven't felt in weeks.

The car's stopped. It's nighttime. They're still there, but they're not moving. We're at that old church, where we buried Peej.

"I think she's awake," I hear Elaine whisper.

"And?"

"Triss, I don't think I can..."

"You don't have to. I'll take care of everything, like always."

I see the shape in the driver's seat place a hand on the shape beside it. There's something rough in it. Something possessive. I cringe at the little gasp that escapes from Elaine's lips. Fog puffs on the window as she trembles a breath.

Triss leans, craning to see something in the graveyard, or maybe in the church.

"What is it?"

"Saw something moving."

"Maybe it's a fox," Elaine says, and I can hear the hope in her voice. The vain hope.

"I'll check it out."

Before Elaine can stop her, Triss pops the door and steps out into the night, pulling her hood up and her jacket tighter around her. Her breath mists like dragon smoke. She stalks across the cemetery, clutching a dagger she must have borrowed from Belladonna. There is no sign of the rolling pin she concussed me with.

I lie in the darkness, listening to Elaine sobbing.

"Elaine," I whisper, once I feel able to speak.

I see her shadow stiffen. I reach for her elbow, but it feels like reaching for a life preserver while I'm caught in a riptide, dragging me under.

"Elaine, please…"

"Stop it, Lori," she squeaks.

"You can't let her do this."

"What am I supposed to do? I can't stop her!"

"Yes, you can."

She shakes her head, curling her arms tight around her body and rocking in her seat. I know she doesn't want this—doesn't want *any of it*—but the only one with the power to stop it now is her.

"I'm sorry," I groan, spitting the taste of iron off my tongue. If anyone ever sprays luminol in here, I'll have made a blood angel. "I was such a bitch to you when we were kids, and you didn't deserve it."

"You were my friend."

"Was I? I used to sit with Anais and Triss and laugh about how shy you were. We used to talk about how you were weak, about how you didn't have what it took. When you asked us to help you hex Triss, we only agreed out of pity. We thought you'd just shrivel up and die on your own. Does that sound like something friends would do?"

"You were right," she says, and my rotten heart breaks in two.

"No," I growl, "we weren't. Don't you get it, Elaine? We were never the good guys. We weren't trying to help you. We weren't trying to help *anyone*. If we hadn't cast that spell, you'd have gotten over it, found someone else, found some*thing* else. And you'd have been better off. We just dragged you down. Me, Anais, Triss, all of us. You were too good for us."

"You're just saying that because..."

"Because I'm going to die?" I laugh. "I don't want to leave any unfinished business behind. I need you to know the truth. You were stronger than us, because all you ever wanted was to be loved and to be left alone. You *deserved* to be loved. You deserved *better.*"

She breathes deep. I can hear my words echoing inside her head, conflicting with whatever Anais and Triss and Belladonna have told her.

Before I can learn what wins out, someone screams. The sound hits me in my stomach, so visceral I almost cry out. Pain and fear, yes, but also a deep, unfathomable grief. The anguish is so much, I forget my own pain and sit up, staring out of the window. I can only assume Elaine is doing the same.

I realize, with horror, that there are two bikes leaning against the churchyard wall. I recognize them.

And I recognize the girl running across the graveyard, leaving a trail of ghost fog and tears behind her. It's Courtney's friend, Mary.

Something happened in that church. Something bad.

Where's her sister?

Dressed in black, I don't even see Triss until she bears the girl to the ground. They wrestle in the dirt for longer than I think should be possible. Triss is strong and furious, but Mary is fighting for her life. I see their four hands twisting and writhing like snakes around the handle of the knife.

Then I see Triss—my friend, my blood sister—drive the blade down. Mary curls around it as it pierces her belly. Triss bunches a fist in her jacket to force it in deeper. I struggle to sit, but I can't keep sight of the girl as she crumples into the dark grass. Any hope I have that she might survive drains out of me when Triss plunges the knife in a second time.

She's being thorough. No witnesses.

They're kids, Triss. Just kids.

I see her wipe the knife off on her jeans. She's going to have to burn it all tonight anyway.

"Oh no!" Elaine gasps, voice quivering, hand rising to cover her mouth. "Oh gods, oh gods, I can't...I can't believe..."

I could say something. I could push Elaine toward the conclusion I want, but I don't. I keep still and silent and let it all sink in for her. What she's seeing just now—her wife, out in the graveyard—is what we are. What we've become. This is the truth with all the glamour stripped away.

Killers.

We watch Triss dragging Mary's body back into the church by her collar. The girl is nothing but an object now. My last impression of her is one of wide, staring eyes and bloody lips. I can't hold out any hope for poor Grace.

Then, stillness. Silence.

Elaine explodes into action. She pulls a flick knife from the glove box and dives between the front seats, slashing the cord off my aching wrists.

"You need to go," she hisses, "right now! Go, Lori! Go!"

"What about—"

"She's my wife." The terror in her voice is like the high strains of a violin before a woman is stabbed in the shower. "I chose this. I have to live with the consequences."

I can't see her face properly in the shadows. All I can see are the tears glistening on her cheeks, the trembling line of her mouth, and two black holes where her eyes would be.

I was right. She really is stronger than us.

"Go back to Shady Acres," she says. "Find Anais. Stop her. Maybe it's not too late. Maybe we can still save…"

Courtney.

I nod. "I will. Elaine, I'm—"

"You already apologized once. That's enough."

We scramble out of the car, wriggling like a pair of rats caught in a trap, and crawl through the dirt, trying to put as much space between us and the graveyard as we can before—

"Elaine?"

I hold my breath. My lungs start burning straight away. Behind me, Elaine is frozen in panic. Triss marches out of the graveyard, footfalls heavy, and stops at the car. She can't see us, but she notices that we're missing.

"You getting cold feet?" she asks. She doesn't sound mad, and that probably frightens me more than anything else. "You know they were going to die anyway. Once Dani has the feet, the Wolf will get them. Like you told her, it's them or us. I thought you understood that," she sighs. Not angry, just disappointed. "It's okay. Once we've got the feet—Anais, Dani and me—we'll fix this. You won't remember a thing. You can go back to being happy. I told you I'd take care of everything, and that's what I'm gonna do."

I reach out for Elaine. I can't leave her here, with Triss. If she doesn't kill her here and bury her with the other girls, if I can't stop Anais and Dani, they're going to lobotomize her. She'll potter around their house in a daze, baking cupcakes and dusting, kissing a mouth that'll whisper only lies, letting herself be touched by hands that killed innocent children.

She shakes me off. I can't see her, but I hear her whisper, "Run!"

And I run. I take off in the direction of town, of Shady Acres, and I don't stop even though it feels like I'm going to tear apart under the strain. Triss gives a yell and takes off after me, and she'd have run me down just like Mary, if it wasn't for Elaine crashing into her, sending them both to the ground.

I see a knife flash in the moonlight, but I can't tell whose.

Then I'm gone.

That cemetery won't be my grave tonight.

CHAPTER 32

THE DEVIL'S DUE

I don't know how I make it back to Shady Acres on foot. I must have run further and faster than I ever did, even at peak health. My heart's pinballing off my ribs so hard I feel like my bones are fracturing and I can't hear over the crackling in my lungs. If I stop, I might just drop dead.

And I can't die. Not yet. I have to stop Anais and Dani. I have to save Courtney.

After everything I've done, everything I've messed up throughout my life, this feels like the most important thing to set right. I wasn't there for Christie, a lifetime ago, and now she's clinging to life by a thread. If I can't protect her daughter, my failure will have cut to the bone.

Fortunately, Anais is easy to find. She's sitting in her Porsche, self-mutilated face lit by the screen of her phone, doomscrolling while she waits for Dani to finish betraying her friends. The wounds she inflicted as part of her ruse are starting to heal, but I know her scars run deeper. She was always more damaged than the rest of us, never comfortable in her own skin. We all fixed the parts of ourselves we didn't like—it was too easy not to—but it was never enough for her.

I don't think she was ever going to find her place. Not the way we set about things. We enabled her, created a monster, and now I don't think we can go back.

I'm not sure if it's my unsteady gait that gives me away or my labored breathing, but she hears me coming and steps out of the car. Even in this crucial moment, she is made up and manicured, styled and dressed to impress. I wonder if it's just for Dani's sake, or if she wants everyone to know that she's Queen Bitch.

I flatter myself and assume it's me she dressed up for. She knows that this is where it ends for us.

"Don't you know when to throw in the towel, Lori?"

"Don't you know when to quit while you're ahead? The kids already did Marty in for you, but that's not enough?"

Anais shakes her head like she's talking to a child. "Didn't Elaine and Triss tell you? It's them or us. The Wolf wants four rabbits, and that's what we're going to give him. Courtney and her little friends, minus Dani, and I guess that makes you number four."

"Yeah, except Triss killed two of them already, Annie."

I still can't believe it, what I saw at the graveyard. The horror of that moment is etched on my soul. We survived the insanity of our teenage years with the help of the magic, and every spell drew us deeper into Belladonna's web. Without their charms, those girls didn't stand a chance.

Is this what life is like without magic? Short and terrifying? No wonder Anais doesn't want to give it up.

Her nose wrinkles, smelling a setback. Then her features turn contemplative. "I suppose it can't be helped. She must have had her reasons. And the magic number is four. Little Courtney, Christie, her cow of a mother, and...wasn't there a boy as well? Maybe you get to live through this after all, Lori. For however long it lasts."

"I'm not going to let you do it."

"Really?" She slips a hand into the pocket of her blazer and slips out a shiny, steel revolver. It's a fashion piece, bling like her sterling silver necklace and Pandora charm bracelet, but I have no doubt it kills just the same. "What choice do you think you have? I mean, you might have gotten away from Triss and Elaine, but you're still just a dying woman, all alone. No magic. Just cancer."

"That's where you're wrong, Annie. I'm a trailer park girl. And this is a fucking trailer park."

When I was a little girl, in one of his more wholesome moments, my daddy told me that boys were disgusting slime. He told me about the kinds of things they'd do to a girl like me if they got the chance, and what I should do to them before they could touch me. By then, I'd already found his stash of *Playboy* magazines and decided he and I had more in common than I thought. But the lesson stuck in my head.

The handful of dirt I scraped from the road leaves a fine layer of grit in Anais's eyes as I scatter it in her face. She recoils, lifting the gun like she's going to start shooting and hope for the best. I grab her wrists and aim the pistol to the sky. The thundercrack of the gunshot rattles my aching wrists.

She wrestles me around. I used to be stronger than her, but now I'm little more than bones and prayers. I know I'm going to lose, so I headbutt her in the nose and kick her between the legs as hard as I can. She's not disgusting slime like a boy, but I bet it still hurts.

She falls back against the door of her Porsche, groaning from her belly, blood slicking her lips. Then she snarls with red teeth and shoves me away. Her stiletto heel stabs through my trainer and pain shoots through me like lightning. In desperation, I fishhook her mouth with my thumb and pull until I feel her healing flesh split all over again.

Her pistol cracks off my skull and I go down in the dirt. She stands over me, breathing hard, blood dripping off her reopened wound onto my face, and cocks the gun a second time.

"It didn't have to be this way, Lori. You could have been with us on this. It could have been like old times, but no, you turned on us. Hell, even knowing that, I was going to end your suffering for you. A needle in the heart. It would have been instantaneous, instead of this lingering shit you're going through. Despite everything, I thought I owed you that. And this is how you repay me?"

I can't breathe, can't speak, so I lift my hand and flip her the bird.

But, like the old song goes, I've got one hand in my pocket.

Anais probably didn't notice that I'm only wearing one sock, or that I'm carrying half a brick in my sweatpants. As she takes aim, I yank my improvised mace out of my sweats and smash her knee with one swing. This is why it always pays to plan ahead. She drops to the ground beside me, and I punt the revolver away as hard as I can.

"Bitch..." she snarls, clutching her leg.

"Takes one to know one," I snicker.

"What the fuck are you doing?" This from Dani, who watches us from beside the Porsche.

That machine probably represents everything she ever wanted for herself in life, and I find that unbearably sad. I wonder if she can be saved, the way I'm certain Anais now can't.

"Did you get them?" my once-best-friend demands.

She lifts her bag and shakes it. "I got 'em, but..."

"Give them to me."

Anais thrusts her hand out. If Dani gives her the bag, if she gets her grubby fingers on those paws, she'll have magic again. All the dirty tricks in the world won't help me then.

"Don't do it, Dani," I beg, hacking phlegm, trying to keep my throat clear enough to speak. "She's already planning on cutting you out. She doesn't care about you. She doesn't care about any-

one. The moment she gets those feet, it's game over for you. If she doesn't leave you for the fucking *demon* that's chasing us, she'll leave you to rot in Shady Acres like she did Courtney's mom.

"Did you know we used to be besties? That's how Anais rewarded the girl who kept her sane through high school. What chance do you think you'll stand? But then, you already figured that, right? That's why you didn't just hand them over."

One of the few weapons left to me is the distrust Anais has inadvertently sown in her wake. She's tried to play everyone off against one another, but only an idiot would trust someone who'd left a trail of broken friendships in her wake. Someone who'd encouraged you to betray your own friend that very night.

Whatever else Dani is, she isn't an idiot.

"What *did* happen between you and Courtney's mom?"

"That's a story for another time, sweetheart," Anais says, trying to inject motherly gentleness into a voice tight with pain and impatience. "Right now, I *really* need you to give me those feet so I can settle things with the weak link here."

"What do you need the feet for? She's dying. Is she really kicking your ass out here?"

"Dani, you're on the precipice of something great here. Don't ruin it."

"Yeah," Dani mutters, looking at her bag, "I am, aren't I? If I'm going to use magic, I need a coven, right? And the stronger the coven, the stronger the magic."

"Exactly."

"But you all fucked up. You and her and the others. You lost the magic. Even when you had it, everything you got was so... small. I don't want small. I'm sick and tired of small. Maybe I should just...go my own way."

She slings the bag onto her shoulder and starts to walk. I can see the lightness in her steps, the giddy thrill of being the one in control, leaving the rest of us to deal with the mess she's made.

Turns out Anais wasn't Queen Bitch after all.

"Get back here, you little shit!" Anais snarls, lunging after her.

She doesn't make it far. Something dark cuts across my vision, something coarse and rugged, something upright and yet hunched. A wolf and a man both, with teeth and claws aplenty. It engulfs Anais's head in its maw and drags her off her feet. She screams into the cavern of its mouth, her noises turning wet and harrowed as it tears her face apart. Her hand waves the gun around, right up until the beast takes it off at the wrist.

It steps on her belly, ripping her, and pins her to the ground. She lies on her back, a quivering mess, as black vapor mists from its jaws. A thick tongue curls from its mouth, licking the first taste of her away. Then it turns savage, digging into her with every claw. It splits her open and spreads her in the dirt, pelting the Porsche with gore.

It reduces Anais to bones and red. Where once a woman lay, there is now only a stain. Anais's manicured hand reaches out to me plaintively, the only part of her still identifiable. I can even see the white band where her wedding ring used to be. Her mangled screams ring in my ears, and I wonder if that's what I'll sound like when it turns me to gelatin too.

I thought we had more time, but no. Time is up.

The thing standing over what used to be Anais stretches out its lupine features into something a little more human, a *lot* more male, and terrifyingly naked. It rises onto two feet and stretches its straightening spine.

"Loretta," it says. Its voice smokes with something terrible and ancient, resonating in my soul, in my blackened, cancer-ridden heart and between my legs.

I freeze like a...

Like a rabbit.

"It is time."

"No," I insist. "Not yet."

Amusement lights in its black eyes. "No?"

"I need to...I need to know that Christie's going to be safe. Her and her whole family. I won't let anything else happen to them. I've done enough damage already."

"The debt has come due."

"You already took Anais. Take me, Triss and Elaine, the way it was supposed to be."

"I cannot."

It's just as I thought. One of them didn't survive the old church. Maybe they both died, bled out next to each other on the unhallowed ground. Either way, like he says, the debt has come due, and we can no longer pay it.

Unless...

"What about Belladonna?"

The Wolf arches an eyebrow. I have piqued its curiosity. I feel like this is not a good thing.

"I tire of her," it says. "I would take her happily, and yet, she has become wise in her years. Her home is warded. It keeps me at bay."

"What if I..." The audacity of what I'm about to suggest takes my breath away. I don't even know if it's possible. "What if I took you inside?"

"That is an offer that cancels all debts. Are you sure you know what you are offering to me?"

I shrug. I don't have the faintest clue. But Belladonna's number was up probably hundreds of years ago. It's not fair if she gets to keep living, gets to keep trading other folk for immortality. All I'm doing is balancing the scales again.

That's what I tell myself.

"Deliver me to Belladonna," it says, "and we have a deal."

"And you promise not to hurt Courtney or anyone in her family? Or, fuck, anyone ever again?"

"As I said, this offer cancels all debts."

I nod. "Fine. Then we have a deal."

I think it smiles. At the very least, it shows more teeth. I try to stand, but it puts a clawed hand on my head and holds me down. It's so strong, I can't struggle free. Instead, it curls black fingers stinking of coal dust and misery into my mouth and starts to stretch open my lips.

The trailer park is silent. No one wants to see what's making those noises. But a curtain twitches gently aside, a pair of inquiring faces take notice. I'm half aware, as it violates me, that the Wolf isn't the only one who's been watching us all this time.

CHAPTER 33

Nothing Else Matters

A loud bang in the distance jolts me awake. One pop, too loud and singular to be a firecracker. It's a gunshot.

I reach for the lamp on my bedside table, knocking things around until I finally tug the cord, and incandescent light floods the room.

Dani's gone.

I know she doesn't have the book. I'm not an idiot, I've hidden it elsewhere. I swing my legs off the bed. I stub my toe on something hard. "Shit!"

In my scramble to turn on the light, I must've knocked the little box onto the floor. I move to place it back onto the bedside table, but something urges me to open it. Why did it appear at my doorstep tonight, of all nights?

I pull the ribbon free. The inside of the box smells of incense. There's a small blue pouch cinched with a drawstring, and a folded note. I unfold the paper. In the same practiced calligraphy that adorned the tag, it reads: *Eventually, the Wolf devours all of his little rabbits. He hunts you as well.*

I pull the cords on the pouch and shake the contents into my palm. It's a leather thong with a small opaque gemstone wrapped in copper wire. A crudely made necklace. It's pretty, in a DIY crafty sort of way, but what does it mean?

Remembering Mary's warnings, I cross the room and slide open the top drawer of my dresser.

My rabbit's foot is gone.

The Wolf devours all of his little rabbits.

It can't be a coincidence. I slip the leather cord around my neck and it's like I've been submerged in a ray of light. My worry and fear remain like an unwanted passenger, but they are no longer in the driver's seat. For the first time since Teeny's overdose, I feel like everything might be okay. I can't be sure of much, but one thing I do know is that whoever sent this talisman is a friend.

After this is over, I'll find out who sent it and thank them, but for right now, there was a gunshot outside my door, and a Wolf is hunting my coven.

I grab my jacket and a flashlight, and peer down the hall. The gunshot didn't seem to have woken Meemaw or Freddie, so I set off, careful to close the door quietly behind me. I don't want her to hear me sneaking out. She has enough worry and disappointment to deal with already.

Dani has all four of our rabbit's feet, and I know she can't use them by herself. Triss told me the day we helped her bury the bodies that there must always be four. If Dani has taken our charms, it means she has three others in mind.

That means the older coven, but not Loretta. She's dying. Hell, they tried to kill her themselves.

I step out onto the porch. There's a lingering smell in the air of metal and musk. My steps are quick and quiet. I keep the flashlight beam low and squint as my eyes adjust to the darkness. Outside the Smith's trailer sits a shiny black car. It almost feels like déjà vu, but it isn't Heather's Audi this time. It's a sports car, an expensive one. It doesn't belong in Shady Acres.

I step closer to the car. The smell is stronger here. As my eyes adjust, I make out the dark stains on the broken asphalt.

I gasp and clutch the talisman hanging around my neck when I recognize the lump of leather and pulp lying beside the car is a person. *Was* a person. Her entrails are scattered over the pile of skin and bloody bone, making the stench of shit and disembowelment temporarily more potent than the animal musk lingering on the breeze. Chunks of hair that have been pulled from the scalp by the roots, bite marks from a huge maw make the face unrecognizable.

Bite marks. Whoever this is, they weren't just killed—they were devoured.

Dani's name is stuck in my throat, but the hair isn't right, and the clothes aren't hers, and who the hell does the car belong to?

The Wolf is real, and if this isn't Dani, then I might not be too late.

I backtrack to grab my bike and realize the lights were on inside the Smiths' trailer. The old ladies must have heard the gunshot. I wonder if they called the police.

I pedal hard, turning onto the trail, heading into the woods. I don't know if I can stop Dani, but I need to try.

I head toward the church because I don't know where else to go. The wind picks up, carrying that familiar animal scent, the one that hangs heavy in the air surrounding Shady Acres tonight. I'm thankful I remembered to grab my jacket.

Beneath the smell I've come to think of as the Wolf, there is something else.

A car sits a short distance from the graveyard. The back door hangs open, interior light spilling yellow into the otherwise dark night. Even the moon seems afraid to show itself tonight. I know this car. I've seen it parked at the Mason House, and later at Anais's house.

I prop my bike against a crumbling gravestone and step slowly, tentatively in the direction of the car. "Hello?"

Silence is the only answer.

"Dani?"

I don't know why I expected her to be here.

My sneakers hit a wet patch on the ground, and I slide, coming down hard on my knees. The acrid stench of vomit hits my nostrils and I realize I've landed in a puddle. I turn, worried I might add to the collection, and then I see the cause.

If the body outside the Smith trailer was bitten and torn, this one was downright mutilated. Whoever—*whatever*—did this had taken its time. Flesh is torn off bone and skin has been peeled from layers of muscle and sinew. The sight forges memories I'll never be able to forget. The chest is caved in, blood smeared across breasts pierced with deep canine cuts.

This is what it looks like when the Wolf devours his rabbits.

"Fuuuuck!" I grab fistfuls of my hair and scream as I tug. *This can't be real. It can't be happening.*

I climb back onto my feet. I have to find Dani, maybe Loretta, if they're still alive. The note says the Wolf devours all and based on the number of bodies I've seen tonight, I can't assume any of us are safe. I start for my bike when a soft groan from the ruins stops me dead in my tracks.

"Hello?" I ask, barely above a whisper. I don't know what I'm more afraid of—if someone will answer, or they won't.

I creep toward the church on high alert, ready to run. I sweep the beam of my flashlight through the darkness and see the trail of red. It stops at a pale hand, wrist wrapped in a Rainbow Loom friendship bracelet.

"Mary?"

Blood is caked in the corners of her mouth, and her eyes stare past me at nothing. Her left arm juts out at an awkward angle, like she'd fallen. She isn't torn apart like the others.

The front of her shirt is ripped, with a dark stain at the

center of her chest. I pull away the fabric. She wasn't attacked by the wolf—she was stabbed. Murdered. A sob tears itself from my throat.

Did the older coven do this? Why?

Mary's dead. But that means...the groan hadn't been her.

"God, no," I moan, and stagger away, frantically searching the ruins of the church.

Grace lies with her head against the stone I'd thought of as our altar. The side of her head is coated in blood. I kneel on the floor beside her. I'd read somewhere that you aren't supposed to move people who've experienced trauma, but I'm not sure if she's alive, so I grab her hand. It's still slightly warm.

"Grace?" The name escapes as another sob. "Grace, can you hear me?"

Her eyelashes flutter, but she never quite opens her eyes. "Court?" her voice is hoarse, like she desperately needs a drink of water.

There's a tearing noise as I pull her head into my lap, cradling it. Blood runs from her head wound, soaking into my pants and jacket. "Yeah, sweetheart. I'm here." I choke on the words.

"The...old..." Her words are broken, raspy things. "They chased..." Her eyes open, and for a split second, she looks directly at me. "Did Mary...get away?"

Every breath she takes sounds like a struggle. I don't see any obvious wounds, like with Mary. Did she fall, or did they bash her head against the altar? And if they stabbed Mary anyway, does it matter?

Tears burn my eyes. Why is everything stacked against us? We're so fucked up, even magic can't help us. Mary's gone, and Grace is going to die.

I hug her against me as best I can. I only hesitate a moment before the lie pushes past my lips. "Yes. Mary got away. She's gone to get help. She'll be back soon." I sniffle, crying into her blood-soaked hair.

Grace was here because I invited her, because we needed a fourth. She'd just wanted to hang out with the older kids, to feel cool.

What kind of monster am I? Like the Wolf, I've taken something innocent and defiled and devoured it. It shouldn't be Grace, the best of us.

She grows still, and the sound of my sobs fill the night.

I don't know how long I stay there, hugging Grace's limp form, before I collect myself. I don't want to leave her, but the night isn't over, and the Wolf is still on the hunt.

Dani might still be alive. I'm not sure where she might be headed, but I follow the musky scent that rides the breeze and hope I'm heading in the right direction.

At first, her form is just another shadow slinking out from under the trees.

"Dani!" Relief washes over me. I realize that I half expected to find her in the same state as the pulped corpse beside the sports car.

She has a sack thrown over her shoulder, and when she turns, I could swear she's happy to see me. But Dani's always been good at showing people what they want to see.

"Court?" she asks. Her forehead is creased into a frown. She glances down at my clothes and her lip curls in disgust.

I bring my bike to a stop three feet from her. I want to tell her I'm happy to see her. I'm glad she's alive. I want to tell her about Mary and Grace, but what comes out is, "You took my rabbit's foot."

She looks down at the dirt caught in the beam of my flashlight. "I'm sorry. I wanted...I thought..."

I can't tell if her expression is actual regret, or only embarrassment that I'm calling her out. "You're going to betray us for the other coven?" I drop my bike and feel a swell of heat rising in my chest.

"I thought they were stronger. I was wrong."

"I thought, you and I...I thought we were something. I thought it meant something."

I bite the inside of my cheek. *I won't cry. I won't cry. I won't cry.*

"Come with me," Dani says. "Mary and Grace are moving, but you and me? We can start over."

"Mary and Grace are dead," I say. "Your friend Anais and her coven killed them."

Dani's eyes widen. She hadn't known. "That doesn't change anything," she says, but there is a familiar flash of anger in her eyes. "It's sad, I know, but the strongest survive. *We survived.* We can be together, and we'll be powerful because we'll really love each other, not like the older coven. They had to cast spells on the people they loved, but it won't be like that between us. I really *do* love you. It'll be perfect."

It's what I've always wanted, for Dani to tell me she loved me. I've hoped and prayed and dreamed of the day when it would happen. But she'd barely reacted when I told her Mary and Grace were dead. Our friends were dead and all she could say was that it didn't change her plans?

Don't cry. Don't cry.

The words on the note invade my thoughts and echo through my skull: *Eventually, the Wolf devours all of his little rabbits,* and I remember Dani's in danger. We're all in danger.

"We have to stop this. It isn't safe. There's something hunting the older coven, hunting us all. I don't know how many of us are left. I think we should destroy the rabbit's feet and be done with it."

Dani shakes her head, but it isn't defiance I see reflected in her features. Her eyes swim with tears. "I need this, Courtney. I'm not gonna rot in Shady fucking Acres."

"Please," I beg. "We'll find another way. Just not this." My voice cracks. *Don't you dare cry.*

Dani turns her back.

"Wait!" I grab her by the shoulder and spin her around.

There are wet streaks trailing down her cheeks. Maybe she did mean it after all. Maybe she does love me in her own way.

"Tell me how to change your mind," I plead. "I'll do anything you ask."

She wipes her face on the back of her sleeve. "Come or don't come, but I won't change my mind."

The truth of her words hits me like a gut punch. Dani's always been this way. Once she sets her mind to something, she rarely changes it. The girl I love is walking away from me, toward God knows what, and there's fuck all I can do about it.

Don't fucking cry.

But there *is* one thing I can do. I reach around my neck and lift the leather cord. I still don't know who left it—whether it was Loretta or one of the other witches who had a change of heart— but someone felt the need to warn us. As soon as the weight of the necklace is gone, the panic and fear set in. Suddenly, I'm a rabbit hunted by a Wolf. I feel him in these woods. He's everywhere.

I desperately want to put the stone back around my neck, I want the feeling of warmth and protection back, but instead, I press it into Dani's hand. "Take this. Promise you'll wear it."

She glances at the talisman.

"Promise!" I shout.

"Okay, I promise."

I press my lips to hers, for what I know will be the last time. She kisses me back, and I can taste the salt of her sadness on my tongue. "Goodbye, Dani. Be careful."

It takes every shred of willpower I can muster to stand in place and not follow as Dani walks away from me. When she vanishes back into the shadows of the night, I turn and head for home.

CHAPTER 34

LIKE A STONE

I remember nothing of the walk from the old church to Shady Acres. By contrast, I remember everything about my slow, lurching march from the trailer park to Belladonna's house. My body feels like it's on fire with every step. Twice, I stop to puke. A stream of black tar ejects from me and smokes wherever it touches. I smell like an ashtray. Like a mine fire.

Finally, I reach the house where it all started. The house where it all ends, I guess. I stagger up the steps, trying not to notice how dark my veins are through my paper-thin skin, or the way my nostrils light up like embers when I suck in a new breath.

I force my way inside without knocking again. I feel something push against me on the threshold. It's like shoving through a chicken wire fence, like I'm cubing myself. The pain cuts right through me, and then I'm standing inside the house, still intact.

At least, I think I am.

The entrance hall is as far as I can go at first, too exhausted to move for a moment. I prop myself against the wall, between landscapes of this region as it used to look, probably in the days when

Belladonna first gained her powers. Then, I drag myself down the corridor, searching for the woman who cancels all debts.

I find her in the parlor, where we whiled away many an afternoon, performed many a ritual. We sacrificed our rabbit here, same as Courtney and her friends. We thought we were unstoppable back then. A force to be reckoned with. Watch out world, here we come.

We were idiots.

She stands at the window, looking out over the world she hasn't set foot in for years. She probably only ventures out when the Wolf is fed and happy, when she doesn't have to fear him running her down like prey. Her dress is funereal black, and she has a veil drawn over her eyes like a widow. Or Morticia fucking Addams. The lace clings to every curve and I am reminded of the crush I've had on her for the better part of twenty years.

Only betrayal has a way of taking the edge off lust.

"You're the last woman standing, Loretta," Belladonna says, without looking around at me. She holds up a glass of wine and I realize there's another resting on the table. For Anais, I assume. "I must admit, I wasn't expecting that."

"I'm full of surprises."

"What happened to dear Elaine and Triss?"

"They had a disagreement about whether it's okay to murder children. I'm inclined to agree with Elaine's view that it isn't."

"Did she finally stand up for what she believed in, after all this time?"

"Yeah, just as soon as she didn't have the rest of us holding her back."

"I'm proud of her."

I scoff. "What about Anais? You proud of her too?"

I wonder how she'll react when she finds out that her most loyal follower now resembles roadkill in the middle of Shady Acres. How will the police justify it? Animal attack? Homicidal

maniac? Industrial accident? I suppose I won't be around to find out, but even I'd struggle to come up with a story credible enough.

"I'm proud of you all. Proud of how you're all fighting for what you desire most. Anais for her livelihood and her power, Triss for love, Elaine for self-respect, even young Dani for a chance to live a better life. But you, Loretta. You've come a long way from where you started."

She walks to her high-backed armchair, where she used to watch us practice our craft, the alpha female we all wanted to be, surveying her domain. Only I've cut through that delicious cake down to the core and all I've found is fear layered on selfishness.

She slides into the chair and folds one long, smooth leg over the other, gestures for me to sit on the couch. I choose to stand.

"The others used the magic to improve their lives. You used magic just to survive. I didn't feel as close to any of them as I did to you. You understood the truth. That it can't be spent on small, petty things. Magic is about life and death."

I nod. After tonight, I know that better than I ever did. The magic has ruined our lives and caused so many deaths.

"I can save you, Loretta."

"How?" I ask, and the word sounds like a plea to my ears.

At that, she laughs a silvery laugh and drains her wine. "Magic. How else?"

"Okay, then why? Why would you save me? I've been working against you all this time."

"Have you? Or have you been working against Anais and her childish schemes? The truth is, you and I are more alike than you believe. You see the bigger picture. And life hasn't been fair to you. Cancer, so young? Ill-fated love? Your parasitic, ugly-minded parents? Friends who betrayed you?"

She leans forward, and I am pinned by the weight of her stare. Through her veil, I see intensity burning in her eyes that I don't think I've ever seen before.

"I'm lonely."

"Huh?"

"Do you know how long I've lived in this house by myself? A long, long time. You guessed already that I'm older than I look. That I don't age the way others do. And, in all that time, I have never had anyone to share this place with. To share *myself* with."

I want to ask her what she's talking about, what this has to do with me, but I'm suddenly speechless. She rises from her seat again, setting the empty glass aside, and rounds the coffee table to lay a hand against my breast. My heart beats against her palm.

"Elaine and Triss had something beautiful, but it wasn't *real*. Your relationship with Christina was always fraught with turmoil. I promise, it wouldn't be the same with me. I see you and love you for who you are. Let me help you, Loretta. Let me save your life, and you can stay here, with me, for as long as you desire. Everything I have will be yours. *Everything...*"

I only realize she's leaned closer when her breath tingles on my lips. I pull back, blinking to dispel whatever she's doing to me. I can't tell if it's magic or just the strength of her desire, but in that moment, all I can think about is Christie.

There's a reason I haven't dated since high school.

"And do what? Help you start another coven? Kill more rabbits? How many more? When does it end?"

"It doesn't have to end, Loretta. It can go on forever if you want it to."

"That's just it!" I scream. "I *don't want it to!*"

Her expression changes in a heartbeat. The softness, the longing, evaporates, leaving only hard, cold steel behind. Hard, cold steel in her hand too, sliding between my ribs. I gasp as the knife sinks deep. Belladonna holds me up, surprising me with her strength.

"Then it's probably better to end it now," she says, "quickly."

She releases me, and I fall to the floor. I bleed on her carpet,

because if she'd put plastic down like she normally does, I might have been suspicious. I am just another rabbit to her, not the partner she tried to convince me I could become. I kneel at her feet, just trying to breathe, and that's how she likes it.

"Maybe Danielle will be more amenable to the offer."

The noise I make is involuntary, a hideous laugh that rattles inside my chest. Only it's not me laughing. I open my mouth and choking darkness pours out, pooling on the floor at Belladonna's feet.

She recoils with a cry of horror and dismay. That might have made me laugh, but the pain of this *thing* forcing its way out of me steals all my thoughts. I retch and retch and retch, hands splayed on the carpet, back arched and heaving. My ribs feel broken, my flanks aching. With one, final heave, I am spent and roll onto my back.

The Wolf unfolds from the swirling darkness. He tasted as bad on the way out as he did on the way in. He flexes, stretches, claiming his full, daunting height. He looms over Belladonna and she backs into the wall, nothing but terror on her beautiful face.

She looks at me and shrieks, "How could you?"

"I was going to ask you the exact same thing," I say.

"The time has come, Belladonna," the Wolf says, voice sonorous, filling the entire house, shaking it to its very foundation.

Belladonna lifts a trembling hand to her mouth. Her eyes blaze with a mixture of white-hot fear and rage. "I won't let you take me," she snarls, defiant to the end.

"You won't have a choice this time."

This scenario plays out in a million different ways in the heartbeat of their hesitation. Every muscle in Belladonna's body pulls taut as she wrestles with all the right and wrong choices she could make. There's a world where she and the Wolf destroy one another in an internecine magical conflagration that razes this house to the ground and takes me with it as ash into the night sky. There's a world where she banishes him into whatever dark, black hole he crawled out of, slits my throat and goes to find her next victims. Maybe there's even a world where I kissed her, and we spent the next four hundred years punishing the world for crossing us.

This is not those worlds.

She lunges to her left. His body flows to intercept her like a shadow across the wall. She swipes at him with the dagger, and he evades with a speed I can't register. Did he even need to? Or is it all part of the game?

Belladonna flees the room, seeking some hidden cache of magic that might turn the tables. It isn't going to help. The Wolf is at her door.

Should I feel bad? I've brought about the doom she's been hiding from for centuries. I am killing something ancient and venerable, something that I should sympathize with, because this is a woman railing against the unfairness of the world, against death itself. A woman with no love for men, who found herself indebted to one anyway.

Except that the bitch stabbed me and planned to let her flunkies kill the only woman I ever loved.

Fuck her.

I lie back and exhale. Once my lungs empty, I can't fill them again. My eyes slip closed and I'm lost in darkness, listening to Belladonna scream and tear apart her own house trying to fight the inevitable. My life leaks through the hole in my chest.

I could save you.

His voice is like another dagger sliding through my heart. It reaches me even at the bottom of the pit I'm sinking deeper and deeper into. I wonder how he has the power to split his attention between me and Belladonna, but he is something older and darker than even her.

"Why would you?"

Those who revere me with sacrifice will be rewarded.

"I don't want what you're offering. I don't want to be like Belladonna."

She was given a gift. What she became was a result of choices that she made, not the gift itself.

I say nothing. I don't have the strength or the will for a philosophical debate with a creature that simply doesn't understand. I sink lower and wonder how much farther there is to go before I hit the bottom.

A quid pro quo then. One good turn deserves another. Surely you have something you desire.

I want nothing from him. Even so, I can't help thinking of my greatest regret. The one, last thing I might wish for.

I think of Christie.

"I want to see her again."

CHAPTER 35

A Life for a Life

I hear the fire eating the house from the ground up and Belladonna screaming, screaming, then silenced. Then all I hear is the gentle beeping of a heart monitor, the muffled paging of Doctor Someone to Ward Somewhere. The stink of chemicals sting my nostrils and my eyelids flutter open to behold the dearest thing I almost lost twice.

Christie lies in the hospital bed that has become her world, eyes closed serenely, hair fanned on her pillow. I figure the nurses must be taking pretty good care of her, or her mom's coming in daily to make her look like an angel in cotton sheets. When she's like this, she doesn't look troubled or traumatized, doesn't look angry or sad or sarcastic. She looks like she did when we were young.

I don't question how I ended up here. Like the Wolf said, one good turn deserves another. I'm getting what I asked for, no strings attached. A chance to see Christie one last time.

I sit forward in my chair. I expect pain from the stab wound in my guts, but there's nothing. A hand to my ribs confirms it.

I am whole and hearty, like I was before I had my run in with Anais in the trailer park. If it wasn't for the burning in my lungs, I would have thought I was going to live.

"I miss you," I tell her, reaching out to take her hand, but I hesitate, afraid she'll turn to smoke and slip through my fingers. "I missed you a lot. I always said you were my biggest regret, but... that's not true. I regretted everything else. You were the one thing I should have never let go."

I've been putting these sentiments into words for years, chapter after chapter, book after book. Whenever one of my characters didn't get the girl, it wasn't the girl's fault. It was mine, reflecting back at me from the laptop screen, from the pages. Bad decisions, stupid mistakes, shitty luck, crystalized into a life that ends with me dying of cancer, all my friends dead, my money run out and a demon the only reason I didn't burn to death in a witch's house.

"Belladonna's gone," I say, wiping my nose on my sleeve. "Anais too. I don't know for sure about Triss and Elaine, but...I think they're both dead. Courtney's going to be okay. Your mom and Freddie too. I...made a deal. To be honest, I think I got the better end of it."

How often could you say that, in this world?

"I probably should have been more specific. I said I wanted to see you again, so this is what I get. Sitting, talking to you while you're out of it. Maybe I should write a letter, but...I've tried that before. I suck at it."

I woman up and slide my fingers into her hand. I'm surprised at the warmth of her skin, but then, she's still alive. Why would she be cold? If either of us is the ghost here, it's me.

"Your mom needs her daughter back. Your daughter needs her mom back. I don't want you to keep self-destructing because of us. We were never worth it. I know things are tough sometimes—hell, a lot of the time—but you were always stronger than

us. You can deal. I know you can."

I thought Christie had lost herself in the drugs and the vain hopes of becoming a rock star, while we had made something of ourselves with our magic. Instead, we were the ones who'd succumbed to our vices—Anais, Triss, Elaine, Belladonna, and me. Whatever else Christie might have done, her greatest victim had always been herself.

"It's funny," I say, and manage a smile. "You know I'm worth more dead now than I am alive? The royalty payments dried up and I spent all my savings, but...when I die, the publisher's probably going to rerelease all my books. My life insurance will pay out."

I've been trying not to think about it, because it's depressing that the best thing I can do for someone these days is die, but I'm not afraid anymore, now that the time has finally come.

"It's for you, Chris. I left it all to you. I couldn't think of anyone else to name as the beneficiary, so..."

So I wrote her name in the box. Didn't even really think about it. To this day, it might be the best decision I've ever made. She's going to be fine. Her family's going to be fine. I hope this helps to balance the scales.

"I should have stayed with you," I whisper, leaning in and touching my lips to her forehead. "I hope you forgive me. I was always just too afraid of how I felt. I could never admit it, even to myself. Even the last few weeks, when you were closer than ever, I couldn't just come out and say it." I gulp down a mouthful of acrid blood and lie back in my seat. My hand slips out of hers and falls, hanging at my side. I can't lift it. "I'm not afraid anymore. I love you, Christie."

I exhale, and when my lungs are finally empty, I find I can't fill them back up again. Whatever life the Wolf had breathed into me is spent. We're quits now. My vision narrows. My eyes flicker closed.

Somewhere, in the darkness, I hear someone whisper my name. I hear them scream it. I hear the rapid bleeping of an emergency button being pushed.

But it doesn't matter. I came here. I said my piece. I saw her again, just the way I wanted to.

And I think—I really do think—that she heard me. She finally heard me say it.

CHAPTER 36

We're All We Have

Grief clings to us like shadows. There's been so much loss, and for what? Maybe Skeet deserved to die, but Mary and Grace didn't.

So many bodies. Almost every member of both covens is dead. The only ones who remain are me, Teeny and Dani. If the cops know who or what did it, they aren't saying. But I know. It was the Wolf.

I can't shake the lingering question: *Am I supposed to be dead too*?

No matter how many questions remain, no one is left to answer them for me.

I hold the screen door open for Teeny, who carries a box full of her junk and places it down in the living room of what used to be Loretta's trailer. Loretta left her everything. Mom decided to move into the trailer and try to make a life for herself.

"Where do you want the keyboard and the amp?" I ask, closing the door behind me.

"The back bedroom," Teeny answers. "We're converting it

into a studio." Despite her grief over Loretta's death, her face has color and has started to fill out again. She didn't cry at Loretta's funeral. She says she's made her peace.

The next box I haul in is full of her old Lisa Frank notebooks. The ones Meemaw shared with me. "What about these?"

She picks one up and flips through with a grin. "I must've been your age when I kept these. Maybe there are some lyrics in here I can recycle." She wipes the sweat off her forehead. "Do you think you might help me with something?"

"I'm helping now, aren't I?"

"I meant more long term." She turns and lifts a brochure off the coffee table, offering it to me. It's for Walnut Grove Community College. She unfolds the pamphlet and holds it out. "They have a music technology program. I learned about it from some of the folks at my AA meetings at the community center. They say I can get financial aid."

My heart speeds up. I can't remember a time when Teeny has thought about her future beyond where to find her next drink.

"The trailer is paid for. Loretta made sure of that. I'm going to get a part-time job. Something good, better than Mudder's Hole. I want to make a life and do something you and Freddie can be proud of."

"You said you needed my help?" I remind her.

She flops down on the sofa. All the furniture is stuff Loretta left behind. The payout from the insurance was substantial, but Teeny's hospital stay took a chunk. She decided to save the rest. There was a time, not long ago, when she would have drunk, snorted and smoked away that whole sum. I hope that day doesn't come again, but if it does, I'll be here for her.

We're all we have left.

"My license got suspended years ago, but I was thinkin' that with some of the leftover money, we could fix your car. I know it's not new or fancy, but it will get us back and forth." She uses

words like "we" and "us", as if there ever had been such a thing.

"Yeah," I answer, swallowing back my emotion. I'll be damned if I let myself get all teary-eyed now. "I can do that."

She smiles and laughs her relief, and I realize she was nervous. She thought I might say no. A month ago, I would have.

I wonder if, now that all the witches are dead, Teeny can finally have peace. But there's still the matter of Dani. I haven't seen her since the night she stole my rabbit's foot and I turned down her offer to reform the coven. I can't help but wonder if the talisman kept her safe.

I study Teeny's face, and while she looks healthier and stronger, I don't think she's ready for the conversation about Dani. Not yet. I need her to stay clean, to make goals, to get her future so firmly on track that she won't fall off the rails at the first sign of an obstacle.

I point to the boxes on the floor. "Why don't you start putting things in the studio? I'll take out the recycling."

I don't say I don't want her to see all the empty liquor bottles that were in the kitchen in case it triggers something. I don't know how recovering addicts work, but a trigger is a trigger, and someone has to watch out for her now.

She nods and lifts a box as I retreat into the kitchen and grab a clear waste bag, unceremoniously dumping a bin of empty bottles inside. The bottles hadn't been empty when Teeny learned she'd inherited the trailer. Meemaw and I had cleaned up the place before Teeny's release from the hospital.

Better safe than sorry.

I walk outside and take the can from the tiny shed in the corner of the lot. The hairs on the back of my neck rise. I'm being watched.

At first, I think it might be Freddie, but a quick glance across the yard reveals nothing. Maybe someone is peeking out a window. All these unsolved deaths have everyone on edge, me included, but there's no obvious threat.

I take a deep breath and inhale a familiar musky scent. I place the can by the street, depositing the bag of empties, slamming the lid down tight.

A low-pitched growl comes from somewhere behind the trailer. I don't think any of our neighbors have a dog. I step forward, not sure whether to walk or run back inside. The sound deepens, coming from the chest, not the throat. The sun is up, there is no darkness to hide behind, but I still see nothing.

When I return to the trailer, Teeny has one of her notebooks open. She's flipping through it and chewing on her lower lip.

"You okay, Mom?"

She glances up and her face brightens. I doubt she can remember the last time I called her mom because I certainly can't.

"There's an extra bedroom. I wonder if you wanna use it. I'm not asking you to move in or anything. Not if you don't want to." She runs a hand through her hair, looking at the scattered boxes rather than meeting my eyes. "Freddie's still little, but you're practically grown. So, I thought you could have the bedroom and come and go as you please."

I temporarily forget about the growling thing outside, and Dani, and bins full of empty bottles. I take a seat on the couch next to Teeny and wrap her in a hug.

"Courtney," she sobs against my shoulder. "I'm sorry I've been such a shit mom."

I inhale her scent. There are no traces of booze or stale cigarettes. She smells like vanilla and hope.

"I love you, Mom."

EPILOGUE

THE CRAFT

She was the victor, the one who had it all figured out. She saw their weakness and knew she was better than any of them. Yes, she lied to her, told her it was love, but lying was an awful difficult habit to break.

The woods had no love for her either. Her tattered sneakers didn't keep the stones and the water out, and the branches caned her back and thighs like every bad daddy her momma ever brought home from the bar. The cold didn't take the edge off her anger. It only made her yearn to punish them more.

The moment she felt far enough away, the moment she felt safe, she threw the bag down on a tree stump and unzipped it. There, inside, were the rabbit's feet, the totems that unlocked the magic. They were supposed to be the key to everything she ever wanted.

But they were rotten. The magic was gone.

Dani tossed the bag in the dirt with a scream. Why, why, *why* did it have to be like this? After everything she'd done to get those feet, this couldn't be how it ended. She couldn't go back.

Courtney wouldn't kill her, but Anais...

She needed magic. Only magic could keep her safe.

Someone was cooking something. A regular, old hillbilly cookout in the woods, clear of Shady Acres. She could smell meat spitting in the open air, roasting on an open fire. Her stomach churned, because she'd skipped dinner, and lunch, and breakfast, and because she'd puked last night trying to work up the nerve to go to Courtney's and steal her foot.

She hesitated, because a man sitting on his lonesome out in the middle of nowhere eating roadkill wasn't likely to have all his dogs barking, but one hunger or another pulled her into the clearing. Something made her pause at the tree line, and she remembered what Courtney had said to her. She'd made a promise, and normally promises were like candy hearts dissolving in the spit of your lies, but she kept this one.

She slipped the necklace around her neck and felt, suddenly, safer. Her lips still burned from where they'd kissed, but regret was chased away by the possibility, if not the actuality, of hope.

The stranger stared at her, all fiery eyes and dark hair and the kinds of muscles she normally only saw in MCU movies. She wrapped her fingers tight around the necklace gem.

"Take a seat," he said. Not a request.

"Who the fuck are you?" she asked, ignoring him.

He smiled the kind of smile that made intelligent women afraid. Dani, who'd been playing dumb most of her life, felt a prickle of terror down her spine and didn't show a lick of it.

"Not who."

"Whatever, man. Have a nice night." She backed out of the clearing, nice and slow, never taking her eyes off him.

His head tilted, sizing her up, like he'd expected this conversation to go differently. "I take it you know the feet are useless now?"

Dani froze. A twig broke under her heel and she flinched.

When he didn't come leaping after her, she stepped closer again. She fixed her features in a glare. He needed to know this was a temporary arrangement. First creeper vibe she got, she was gone. "What do you know about it?"

"I gave magic to those objects. They are symbols of power, yes, but the power is mine."

"Yeah, no problem, Captain Planet. So, what, you had a deal with Belladonna?"

"I did."

"And the reason they're not working anymore is because..."

"Belladonna is dead." He reached forward to lift a spit from the fire, with what looked like a rabbit skewered on it. "I ate her."

He offered the rabbit to her. She held up a hand in disgust, afraid she was going to yack. If she got hungry, she'd just head to McDonalds. They hadn't canceled Skeet's credit card yet.

"You are unlike Belladonna," the stranger said, and he stripped the entire rabbit from its spit, bones and all. "And yet, like her in many ways. Creatures of hunger and fear."

Dani scoffed, not because it wasn't true, but because she thought it was obvious. Wasn't everyone hungry? Wasn't everyone afraid? They were the only really true things in the world.

The only question was, what were you willing to do to feel satisfied? To feel safe?

"Can you give me magic or not?" she demanded, patience fraying.

At this, he laughed. "I can. But you're going to need four rabbits."

THE END.

ABOUT THE AUTHORS

NOTES & ACKNOWLEDGMENTS

Holley Cornetto is a writer, librarian, professor, book reviewer, and transplanted southerner who now calls New Jersey home. Her debut novella, We Haunt These Woods, was released in 2022 from Bleeding Edge Books. Her short fiction has appeared in magazines such as Daily Science Fiction, Flame Tree Press Newsletter, Dark Recesses Press, and anthologies from Cemetery Gates Media, Eerie River Publishing, Dark Ink, and several others. In 2020, she was awarded a grant from the Ladies of Horror Fiction. In addition to writing The Horror Tree's weekly newsletter, she regularly reviews for Publisher's Weekly and The Horror Tree. She teaches creative writing in the online MFA program at Southern New Hampshire University. Find her on Twitter @ HLCornetto.

S.O. GREEN

S.O. Green (they/them) is a fantasy, science-fiction and horror writer living in the Kingdom of Fife with husband, John. They are the chief contract editor and contest judge for Eerie River Publishing. Their cross-generational, all-girl, post-apocalyptic road trip novelette, Sin Chaser, came out in 2021, also published by Eerie. They have over 80 short works published with imprints including Dragon Soul Press, Black Ink Fiction and Nordic Press. They are a writer, vegan, martial artist, gamer and occasionally a terrible person (but only to fictional people).

HOLLEY'S ACKNOWLEDGMENTS:

This book wouldn't exist without Simone Green. I first met Simone a few years ago, and somehow the two of us clicked. I thought Simone's writing was excellent, and through the power of social media, someone I wouldn't otherwise have known suddenly became a friend. When Simone asked me if I was interested in working on something together, I was thrilled with the prospect. My biggest thank you is to Simone, for believing in this story, helping bring it to life, and making it something truly special. You were so easy to work with and so gracious to put up with my barrage of messages and late-night plot notes and questions. We're totally going to do this again, aren't we?

I also want to thank Michelle River of Eerie River Publishing. Michelle is an amazing human, and a great person to work with. She works tirelessly to support her authors and her press, and she makes some of the most beautiful books I've ever seen. Seriously, take a look at her interior formatting. She always goes above and beyond. I couldn't be happier that this series found a home at Eerie River, and that's exactly what it feels like –home.

I also owe thanks to Chris Cornetto, my better half, beta reader, and sounding board. One of the greatest things about being married to a writer is that when you hit a wall, you have an auxiliary brain to tap into to help solve your plot problems. Also, thank you for asking the folks at Panera for hot coffee, it really is gross when it's cold.

A special thank you goes out to Austin Shirey, who reads everything I write before I send it anywhere. He believed in this project from the outset and has always been a source of encouragement when I needed it most.

And lastly, thank you, dear reader, for picking up this book and taking a chance on a bunch of trailer park girls. I hope you love them as much as I do.

SIMONE'S ACKNOWLEDGEMENTS:

Before anything else, I need to thank my partners for their unending support, inspiration and belief, as well as their unflinching acceptance of the fact that I could never be a normal person with normal interests. You make everything better, everything worthwhile, everything possible.

They say you should write the book you want to read. Holley Cornetto gave me that opportunity when she agreed to co-author this novel with me. That there was ever a time when this story, these characters, weren't a part of me seems surreal, but this was Holley's creation first. I am only thankful to her for bringing me along for the ride.

Thanks to my boss, the amazing Michelle River, for so readily agreeing to publish our book, thus adding another plate to her ever-growing collection of spinning dishware. I couldn't be happier with where our story ended up, and where it might still go with Eerie River Publishing's help. If you are reading this book, it is because Michelle put it in your hands.

A huge thank you to the 90s for providing most of the inspiration for this book, as well as a good portion of the anger I channelled into Loretta. A special mention should go to the

late Chris Cornell, and the poignancy of the song Like a Stone, which became Loretta's swansong.

Finally, thanks to you, our reader, for helping this book achieve its true purpose. If you enjoy it, that's all that matters.

AUTHOR NOTE

HOLLEY

This story is a result of a mixture of influences in my life. My experiences as a child in rural Alabama inevitably shape everything I write in some way. The culture I grew up in was steeped in fundamentalist religious tradition and belief. I never really fit in, and I rebelled by watching movies like The Craft and listening to bands like Marilyn Manson. I was the weird kid who sat in the back of French class, reading the novelization of the X-Files. I still can't conjugate verbs, but my love of reading and stories has remained intact over the years.

From the perspective of a reader, I've always loved coming-of-age fiction. Stories about kids stumbling into adult situations, largely unprepared, but somehow finding a way through have always held appeal. Robert R. McCammon's Boy's Life, Stephen King's It, and Dan Simmon's Summer of Night all became the type of stories I wanted to tell. Where this book differs is by offering a female perspective, and a queer one at that. While horror continues to grow more inclusive, there is still more room for female and queer voices in the genre, and I hope Courtney's story helps fill that gap.

Perhaps the biggest influence for this book came from the 1996 movie, The Craft. I was thirteen when this movie was

originally released, and I found myself conflicted by my feelings for Nancy as portrayed by actress Fairuza Balk. I was completely entranced by this character and felt simultaneously compelled by and wary of her. What would it be like to love someone like Nancy? I carried that question with me for a long time, and I think Courtney's relationship with Dani is my attempt to answer that question.

I guess you can say that Simone and I have written the story I most wanted to read. Thirteen-year-old Holley might have been too young for it, but she likely would have read it anyway.

More from Eerie River

Eerie River Publishing, is a small independant publishing house that is devoted to uplifing Indie Authors and releasing quality dark fiction novels, novellas and anthologies.

To stay up to date with all our new releases and upcoming giveaways, follow us on Facebook, Twitter, Instagram and YouTube. Sign up for our monthly newsletter and receive a free ebook Darkness Reclaimed, as our thank you gift.

https://mailchi.mp/71e45b6d5880/welcomebook

Interested in becoming a Patreon member?
Patreon membership gives you exclusive sneak peeks at upcoming books, early chapter releases, covers art as well as free ebooks and discounts on paperbacks.

https://www.patreon.com/EerieRiverPub

HELLULAND

A NOVEL

A GIFT AWAKENING
A LEGEND REVEALED

C.R. LINDSTRÖM

THE VOID

BOOK ONE OF THE FANG RIPPER SERIES

NEEN COHEN

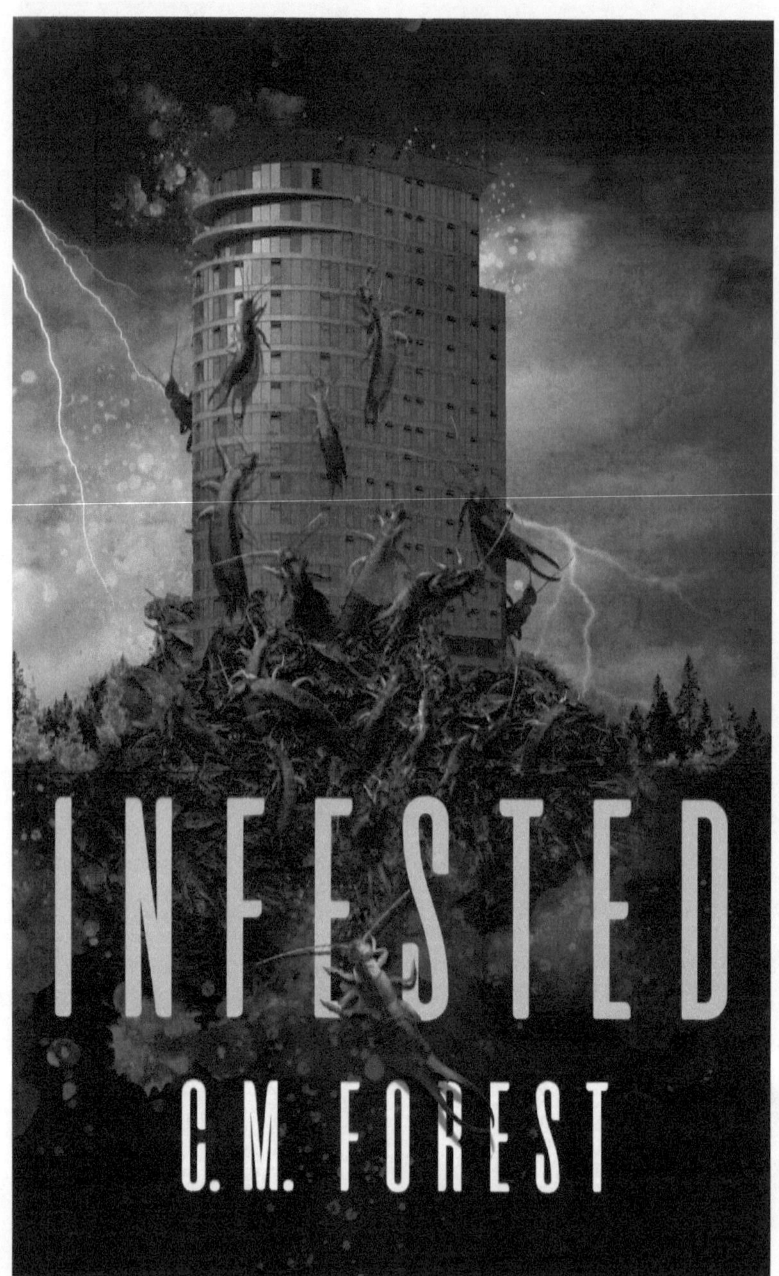

INFESTED
C.M. FOREST

EMPIRE OF RUIN
1
IN SOLITUDE'S
SHADOW
DAVID GREEN

EERIE RIVER PUBLISHING HORROR
BLOOD SINS
BEWARE THE SINS OF THE FATHER
EDITED BY
HOLLEY CORNETTO & S.O. GREEN